The
Second
Chance
Convenience Store

The
Second
Chance
Convenience Store

A Novel

Kim Ho-Yeon

Translated by Janet Hong

HARPER PERENNIAL

NEW YORK • LONDON • TORONTO • SYDNEY • NEW DELHI • AUCKLAND

HARPER ● PERENNIAL

Originally published as 불편한 편의점 in South Korea in 2021 by Namu Bench.

FIRST US EDITION

Designed by Jackie Alvarado

Library of Congress Cataloging-in-Publication Data has been applied for.

ISBN 978-0-06-335477-7 (pbk.)

25 26 27 28 29 LBC 5 4 3 2 1

The
Second
Chance
Convenience Store

The Ultimate Feast Lunch Box

The train was passing Pyeongtaek when Mrs. Yeom Yeong-sook realized the little bag that should have been in her overnight case was missing. She was supposed to be in Busan today, but how could she go without her wallet? The problem was that she couldn't remember where she'd lost it. More than anything, it was her forgetfulness that upset her. She broke out in a cold sweat, frantically retracing her steps in her mind.

She'd still had it when she bought her KTX train ticket at Seoul Station. How else would she have paid for the ticket without getting her credit card from her wallet, which she always kept in her little bag? After that, she'd sat in the waiting room in front of the TV screen for half an hour, watching the twenty-four-hour news channel. On the train, she'd dozed off while clutching her overnight bag, and when she woke up, everything had been exactly as it was. It was only at that moment, as she was retrieving her cell phone, that she realized her little bag was gone. At the thought that all her important items were inside—wallet, bank book, and notebook— she could hardly breathe. Urging the gears in her head to keep up with the racing train, she revisited her memories, trying to rewind the day.

When she kept shaking her leg and mumbling to herself, the middle-aged man sitting next to her cleared his throat loudly. However, it wasn't him but her cell phone ringing from inside her bag that broke through her panic. The ringtone was an ABBA song, but she couldn't recall the title. Was it "Chiquitita" or "Dancing Queen"? *Oh, Junhui, maybe your granny does have dementia after all.* Only when she'd pulled out her phone with shaking hands did the title finally come to her: "Thank You for the Music." Right then on her call screen, she saw an unfamiliar number with an 02 Seoul area code. She took a deep breath and answered.

"Hello?"

No one spoke on the other end, but she could tell by the background noise that the caller was in a public area.

"Excuse me, but who's this?" she asked.

"Is th-this . . . Yeom . . . Yeong-sook?"

She struggled to understand his hoarse mumble. If a bear were to emerge from a cave after a long winter sleep and speak, she imagined it would sound like this.

"Yes, speaking."

"Your . . . w-wallet."

"Oh, yes! You found it? Where are you right now?"

"Seoul . . ."

"Where in Seoul? Are you at Seoul Station, by any chance?"

"Yes . . . S-s-seoul Station."

She heaved a sigh of relief and cleared her throat.

"Thank you for calling. I'm on the train right now, but I'll get off at the next stop and head right back. Can you hold on to it for me or leave it with someone? I'll be sure to compensate you as soon as I get there."

"I'll stay here . . . Got nowhere to go."

"I see. Where should I meet you?"

"Wh-where you take . . . the airport express . . . by GS Convenience . . ."

"Thank you. I'll be there as soon as possible."

"No need . . . to rush."

"All right. Thank you."

When she hung up, she felt a little funny. His slurred, raspy voice suggested he'd been drinking. She wondered if he might be one of the unhoused men who hung out near the station, especially given what he'd said about having "nowhere to go." The fact that he was calling from an 02 number—likely a pay phone—also seemed to confirm he had no cell phone of his own. Suddenly she felt nervous. Although he was returning her wallet, she couldn't shake the feeling that he might want more than the reward she was offering. Still, she reminded herself, it was doubtful someone who would go out of his way to return her wallet would harm her. Giving him the 40,000 won in her wallet as a thank-you would be more than enough. Just then, Cheonan Station was announced as the next stop, where she could switch to return to Seoul Station. Mrs. Yeom placed her phone back in her overnight case and stood up.

As her return train passed Suwon, her phone rang again. She checked the caller ID, chanting the lyrics of "Thank You for the Music" under her breath, as if warding off dementia. It was the same 02 number. She answered, trying to ignore her unease.

"I . . ." he began in his defeated voice.

"Yes, go on," she urged. She heard herself using the same stern tone from managing students years earlier.

"Ma'am . . . I'm h-hungry . . . A lunch box . . . from the store . . . Is it okay?"

Her heart warmed instantly. Her suspicion melted away at the words *ma'am* and *lunch box*.

"Sure, get yourself a meal. And why don't you get a beverage, too, since you must be thirsty."

"Th-thank you."

Shortly after she hung up, a notification for a card charge appeared on her phone. It had happened very quickly. He must have been standing at the store counter when he'd called. His hunger solidified her belief that he was indeed homeless. Reviewing the charge, she noted the details: GS CHAN HO PARK THE ACE LUNCH BOX 4,900 WON.

So, he didn't splurge on a beverage. At least he has some restraint.

She had considered asking someone to accompany her for safety but decided against it. At seventy, despite showing symptoms of dementia, she still had faith in herself. Throughout her teaching career, she had never been timid, handling all kinds of students with confidence right up until the day she retired. She would trust herself now too.

At *Seoul Station* she immediately located the escalator leading down to the airport express trains. As soon as she descended, she saw a GS Convenience to her right and a man hunched over by the entrance, his face buried in a lunch box. She grew nervous as each step brought him more clearly into view. He had a mop of long, matted hair and wore a thin windbreaker and cotton trousers so dirty she couldn't tell if they were beige or brown. There he was, gingerly picking up a cocktail sausage with chopsticks and putting it into his mouth. She was right. He was homeless. Steeling herself, she walked toward him.

As she approached, three men appeared suddenly and rushed toward him. Mrs. Yeom was so shocked she stopped in her tracks. The men pounced on him, pinning him to the ground, trying to snatch something from his hands. She looked around frantically, but those passing by merely cast brief glances, indifferent to a scuffle among homeless people.

The man dropped his food and curled up to protect himself, but the others choked him and forced his arm up, wresting away what he'd been holding. Mrs. Yeom, who had been watching anxiously, caught a glimpse of the object. It was her pink bag!

The three attackers kicked the man several times before starting to flee. Mrs. Yeom's hands and legs trembled so violently that she collapsed to the ground. Just then, the man got up and lunged at the one holding the bag, launching a counterattack.

The man shouted, wrapping his arms around the thief's legs and knocking him down. As soon as he smashed the thief to the ground and yanked the bag out of his hands, the other two jumped on him. In that moment, fury overtook Mrs. Yeom. She sprang up and charged at them, yelling, "You bastards! Let go of that this instant!"

They froze at her sudden appearance. She raised her overnight bag and brought it down on the first thief's head. When he yelped in pain, the other two started backing away.

"Thieves! They're stealing my wallet! Stop them!"

At Mrs. Yeom's shrieks, people finally began to pay attention. They stopped to stare, and the thieves ran off. Only the lunch-box man remained on the ground, curled up in fetal position, clutching the bag. She approached him.

"Are you okay?"

He lifted his head to gaze up at her. With blood and snot running from his nose, eyes swelling from punches, and a mouth hidden beneath a scraggly beard, he resembled a caveman returning injured from a hunt. He slowly sat up, seeming to realize only then that his attackers were gone. She fished out a handkerchief and crouched in front of him. A musty stench hit her nostrils. Holding her breath, she offered him the handkerchief, but he shook his head and wiped his nose with his jacket sleeve. She worried he would get blood and snot on her pink bag, then grew frustrated at her own shallowness.

"Are you sure you're okay?"

He nodded, examining her carefully. Under his scrutiny, she felt nervous, as if she'd done something wrong. She wanted to leave as quickly as possible. It was time to retrieve her bag and be on her way.

"Thank you. For keeping it safe," she said.

He plucked the bag out from under his arm and held it out to her. But just as she reached for it, he pulled it back. He studied her carefully as he opened the zipper.

"What do you think you're doing?"

"You sure . . . you're the owner?"

"Of course I am. That's why I'm here. Don't you remember talking to me on the phone?"

Her mood was on the verge of souring at his absurd suspicion. Without saying another word, he dug inside, found her wallet, and took out her ID.

"Your n-name . . . and birthday."

"You think I'm lying right now?"

"I have to . . . m-make sure . . . I have a . . . responsibility . . . to return it."

"Why don't you check my picture? It's right there on the ID."

He blinked his puffy eyes, glancing from her to the ID. "It d-doesn't . . . look like you."

Stunned, she clicked her tongue, not even angry.

"The picture is . . . too old," he added.

It was an old picture all right, but her face should have been easily recognizable to anyone, which meant that there was something wrong with the man's vision. Or that she'd aged beyond recognition.

"So w-what's your . . . birthday?"

She heaved a short sigh and exaggerated each syllable. "July twenty-fifth, 1952. Happy?"

"Good, good . . . I've got to m-make sure, don't I?"

Looking at her as if he wanted her to agree, he slipped the ID back into her wallet, the wallet into the bag, and handed the bag to her. As the chaos finally settled, gratitude swept over her. He had kept her valuables safe, even while being assaulted by those thieves, and had even verified her identity to ensure she was the rightful owner. It was clear he took his responsibility seriously.

The man rose to his feet with a groan. She also stood and fished out 40,000 won.

"Here," she said, holding out the bills. When he didn't reach for the money, she insisted. "Take it."

Instead, he thrust his hand into his jacket pocket and pulled out a crumpled ball of tissue. He wiped his bloody nose with it, then turned and started walking away. She stared after him for a long time, the bills still in her outstretched hand. He tottered to the front of the store where he'd been eating earlier and squatted on his heels. She followed him.

He was mumbling to himself, gazing at the contents of the lunch box scattered on the ground. She heard him groan. Eventually, she bent down and tapped his back. When he turned, she softened her expression, the same one she'd always used to console timid students.

"Hey, mister, can you come with me for a bit?"

As soon as they stepped out onto the street, the man shrank back, more comfortable in the safety of the station. She gestured to him, urging him forward, and finally got him to leave Seoul Station. They walked in silence along the streets of Garwol-dong. He followed, staying a few paces behind, as she shuffled toward Cheongpa-dong. She wondered why she'd asked him to come with her.

She wanted to repay him somehow, this man who had refused his rightful reward, for keeping her bag safe and for doing the right thing despite his circumstances. More than anything, as a lifelong Christian, she wanted to be a Good Samaritan to this man, just as he'd been to her.

Fifteen minutes later, they left the drab streets around Seoul Station, and a large, ornate church came into view. Students from the nearby women's college, dressed in jeans and jackets, walked past them giggling, while a long line stretched in front of a fast-food joint that had blown up after being featured on TV. Mrs. Yeom looked back to find the man glancing about in bewilderment. Some people avoided them, keeping a wide berth. She felt both anxious and curious about what the passersby might be thinking. After all, Cheongpa-dong was her neighborhood and also where her business was located. She had a reputation to keep up.

Nevertheless, Mrs. Yeom led the man toward Sookmyung Women's University, past two side streets, and arrived at a three-way intersection. The convenience store at the intersection was her business, where she could offer him a new lunch box. She opened the door and gestured for him to come inside. He hesitated and then followed her in.

"Hello! Ah, you're back already?"

Sihyeon, one of her part-time employees, put down her cell phone and greeted Mrs. Yeom with a smile. Smiling back, Mrs. Yeom noticed the girl's face stiffen.

"It's okay. He's a customer."

Sihyeon peered at the man, narrowing her eyes. The girl still had much to learn. Mrs. Yeom guided him by the arm toward the lunch box cooler. He followed without a word.

"Pick one. Anything you'd like."

He looked at her in confusion, but remained silent.

"This is my store, so don't feel bad. Just pick one."

"Then . . . uh . . . huh?"

"What's wrong? Don't you like any of them?"

"But there's no . . . Chan Ho P-Park lunch boxes."

"This isn't GS Convenience. Only GS sells those. We have plenty of tasty lunch boxes too."

"But . . . Chan Ho Park ones . . . are the best."

Baffled by his fixation on a competitor's product, she picked up the largest lunch box from the cooler and handed it to him.

"Try this. The Ultimate Feast. It comes with a lot of banchan."

Holding the lunch box, he carefully counted the number of sides. *That's twelve items, you rascal. A royal spread!* she said in her head, as she watched him study the contents. Once he finished his inspection, he looked up, bowed deeply to her, and then headed outside to the green plastic patio table, as if it were reserved just for him.

The patio table soon became his private spot. Mrs. Yeom watched him open the lunch box lid as if handling a precious object, carefully break apart the disposable chopsticks, and shovel some rice into his mouth. She went back inside to fetch a cup of doenjang soup, setting it on the counter. Quick as usual, Sihyeon scanned the bar code without question. Mrs. Yeom poured hot water into the cup, got a spoon, and headed back outside.

"Here. It's better with soup."

He glanced from her face to the doenjang soup she placed on the table. Before she could hand him the spoon, he raised the cup to his lips and drank nearly half, seemingly unfazed by the scalding liquid. Nodding in satisfaction, he resumed eating.

Mrs. Yeom sat across from him, watching him eat. He reminded her of a bear with a jar of honey. It was probably difficult for a homeless person to eat three meals a day, so how did this man manage to be so big?

"Easy there, slow down. No one's going to steal your food."

He looked up at Mrs. Yeom, grease from the stir-fried kimchi smeared across his mouth. His eyes, no longer guarded, appeared meek.

"It's ... good." He glanced at the lid. "It really is ... the u-u-ultimate ..."

Instead of finishing his sentence, he bowed to her once more and took another sip of soup. He seemed much calmer now that his stomach was full. Mrs. Yeom felt a strange sense of satisfaction watching him eat. She noticed a quiet dignity in his struggle to pick up the last few pieces of fish cake.

"From now on, come here when you're hungry. You can have a lunch box anytime."

He looked wide-eyed at her, his chopsticks frozen in midair.

"I'll let the employees know. You don't have to pay for it."

"The e-expired ones?"

"No, the new ones. Why would you eat something that's expired?"

"The workers ... they eat expired ones ... I don't m-mind."

"Nobody eats expired food here, not the workers, and not you. Have the fresh ones. I'll make sure everyone knows."

He considered it for a long moment, then bowed again without responding and went back to picking up the fish cake. Only then did Mrs. Yeom remember to hand him the spoon she was holding. He stared at it for a few seconds, as if unsure what it was for. Finally, he used the spoon to scrape together the remaining pieces, the muscle memory returning like the act of riding a bike, and, with contentment, brought the spoon to his mouth. After polishing off the lunch box, he looked up at Mrs. Yeom.

"That was good ... th-thank you."

"I should be the one thanking you for keeping my bag and wallet safe."

"They stole it, y-you know . . . There were two of them."

"Two of them?"

"So I gave them a b-beating and got it . . . The pink bag with your w-wallet . . ."

"You mean you got my bag from those thieves? Just to return it to me?"

He nodded and sipped the water she'd brought him. "I can h-handle two . . . but three's h-hard . . . I'll t-teach them a lesson n-next time," he said, gritting his teeth.

She cringed at the sight of the chili pepper flakes stuck between his yellow teeth, but more than that, she was impressed with his bravery.

He finished his water and glanced around. "Wh-where are we?"

"Oh, we're in Cheongpa-dong. Green Hills."

"Green Hills . . . It's nice here."

A corner of his mouth turned up in a smile under his thick beard. He picked up the empty containers and got to his feet. With practiced ease, he tossed them into the recycling bin, then stood before her again, pulling a wad of tissue from his jacket to wipe his mouth. After bowing deeply from the waist, he left.

She watched him walk back in the direction of Seoul Station, like an office worker heading home after a long day. As soon as she stepped back inside the store, Sihyeon fired off question after question, with eyes full of curiosity. Mrs. Yeom recounted everything, from the moment on the train when she realized her bag was missing to now. Throughout the story, Sihyeon interjected with astonishment and concern.

"He's an interesting character—a man of principle. It's hard to believe he's homeless."

"I don't know, Boss. He looked like just another homeless person to me . . . Did you check to see if anything's missing?"

She opened the pink bag. Everything was in place. She smiled at Sihyeon, as if to say "I told you so." Suddenly, she took out her ID and held it up to the girl's face.

"Be honest. Do I look different to you?"

"No. Except for a bit of white hair, you haven't aged at all."

Mrs. Yeom peered closely at her photo. "He's right."

"Pardon me?"

"Yup, he's a man of principle all right." She laughed. "And you're too nice."

She told Sihyeon to give him a lunch box if he came to the store and to inform the rest of the staff to do the same. Although Sihyeon didn't look too pleased, she began typing the boss's instructions into the group chat. Mrs. Yeom glanced around the store with satisfaction, but her heart sank when she realized she couldn't recall any of the customers who had come in while she was dealing with the man. The thought that she might indeed have dementia left a bitter taste in her mouth. Nevertheless, she had received kindness and given it in return. She decided to consider it a decent day.

Sihyeon cleared her throat politely. "But Mrs. Yeom, aren't you supposed to go to Busan?"

"Aigo, what am I thinking?" Her cousin's funeral!

The day was far from over. She still needed to get to Busan, even if it meant arriving late at night. After the funeral, she planned to stay a few extra days, since she was already making the trip. She stuffed the pink bag safely back into her overnight case and headed for Seoul Station once more.

After spending five days in Busan, Mrs. Yeom returned home, stopped by Always Convenience, and found Sihyeon ringing up drinks for a couple. Sihyeon greeted Mrs. Yeom with a glance and came out from behind the counter after the customers left.

"Boss, that man's been coming here every day. He hasn't skipped a day."

"Who are you talking about? The homeless man?"

"Yeah, he comes at the same time every day. He eats a lunch box and then leaves."

"So he doesn't come during the other shifts?"

"No, just during mine."

"Maybe he likes you."

Sihyeon looked appalled and narrowed her eyes. Mrs. Yeom laughed and took the girl's indignation in stride.

"He always shows up at eight p.m., right when we're supposed to throw out the expired food."

"What? I told you to give him a fresh one."

"I tried. I offered him a new one, but he insists on eating the expired ones."

"But I promised him a new one . . . If he eats expired food, that makes me a liar."

"It's tough, Boss. He parks himself in front of the counter, mumbling and stinking up the whole place. One time, a customer walked in, saw him, and walked right back out. What am I supposed to do? Giving him what he wants is the fastest way to get him to leave. Plus, I have to air out the store every time."

"Whew. Okay."

"He comes at eight on purpose. I don't know how he figured it out, but he knows when we toss the expired food."

"I knew it. He's a man of principle."

"I got worried yesterday when he was late. Thought maybe he was sick or something."

Seeing Sihyeon bite her lip in worry, Mrs. Yeom chuckled again. "Sihyeon, you're too soft. How will you get through life?"

"That's funny, coming from you," Sihyeon rebutted. "Who came up with the idea to give him a lunch box every day? What if he brings all his friends here?"

"He's not the type to do that."

"How do you know?'"

"I'm a good judge of character. Why do you think I hired you?" she said, winking at Sihyeon.

"Touché, Boss."

She always enjoyed her conversations with Sihyeon, who was like a daughter to her in many ways. She hoped Sihyeon would pass her civil service exam soon and move on, but the thought of the girl leaving also made her sad.

The door chime signaled a customer's arrival, and Sihyeon returned to her post behind the counter. Mrs. Yeom walked around the store and inspected the lunch boxes. One of these days, she decided, she'd drop by at 8:00 p.m., right at food disposal time. She planned to ask for his name then.

That evening, Mrs. Yeom nodded off while watching television and was startled awake when her phone rang. The time was midnight. Feeling a surge of frustration, she answered and heard the drunken voice of her son. He had no idea she'd gone to Busan, or that her birthday was the next day, but that didn't stop him from professing his love and regret at not being a better son. Predictably, his spiel led into pointed questions about Always Convenience. She told him it wasn't his concern, and as usual, he pitched another grandiose scheme, suggesting she sell the struggling store and invest in his business instead. He claimed she'd have less to worry about and her life would be so much easier. Losing patience, she decided to be blunt.

"Minsik. You shouldn't trick your own mother."

"Mom, don't you trust me? Do you really think I'd do that to you?"

"As a retired history teacher, let me tell you something. People and nations are always judged by their past actions. Reflect on what you've done so far. Would you trust yourself if you were in my shoes?"

"Jeez, Mom, that's not fair. Aren't we family? Why do you all treat me like this? Why?"

"If you're drunk and just want to fight, hang up."

"Mom—"

Mrs. Yeom hung up herself and stormed into the kitchen. Her heart burned, as if on a hot grill. Sharp pain radiated from her chest. She opened the fridge, grabbed a beer, and gulped it down, attempting to extinguish the internal fire, only to end up coughing violently as the beer went down the wrong way. She felt pathetic, resorting to alcohol to drown out her son's words.

What should I do?

She had always tried to live her life with sound judgment and purpose, but her son's troubles constantly threw her off-balance. If she sold the store to fund his latest venture or scheme and ended up losing everything, what then? Her only remaining asset was this old two-bedroom condo on the third floor of a faded low-rise that had stood in the hills of Cheongpa-dong for the past twenty years. Her son's failures wouldn't end until he swallowed up her last asset: this place that was supposed to be her final haven.

It pained her to admit it, but her own son was a fool and a fraud. His ex-wife must have seen the truth, as she filed for divorce after less than two years of marriage. Initially, Mrs. Yeom had been angry at her daughter-in-law's apparent heartlessness, but she soon came to accept the fact that her son was mostly to blame. It took him only three years after the divorce to lose all his money, becoming more pitiful with each passing day. And now, when only a mother could help, what was she doing? She was concerned about a homeless person from Seoul Station, wondering if he had enough to eat, rather than looking after her own son, who was out in the world, drunk and struggling to survive.

She finished her beer and began to pray at the kitchen table. Prayer and petition were all she could do.

Mrs. Yeom spent her birthday with her daughter, son-in-law, and granddaughter, Junhui, who was her pride and joy. This time, her daughter's family didn't come to Cheongpa-dong but invited her to a fancy Korean BBQ restaurant in their neighborhood. Both she and her daughter's family lived in Yongsan, but their neighborhoods were worlds apart. Although Yongsan had become Seoul's second most expensive district after Gangnam, Mrs. Yeom's Cheongpa-dong remained a humble area, filled with old villas packed together and boardinghouses for college girls. Her daughter and son-in-law often talked about saving enough to move to Gangnam's most affluent neighborhood by the time Junhui started middle school. Mrs. Yeom sometimes wondered which of the two was more responsible for their ambitious financial goals and savvy housekeeping, as these sharply contrasted with her own fiscally conservative views. She came to realize that their success was the result of the couple's unique synergy. Her daughter had changed significantly since getting married. Even their conversations had shifted, to the point where her daughter felt less familiar and her son-in-law more aloof. Of course, she worried less about her very capable daughter than her divorced son. Still, Mrs. Yeom sensed that the distance between her and her daughter would only grow once the couple moved to Gangnam.

And now here they were, celebrating Mrs. Yeom's birthday with prime Korean beef at an upscale restaurant. To be honest, she found it somewhat uncomfortable. They used to always get baby back ribs near Sookmyung Women's University in her neighborhood. Feeling awkward, Mrs. Yeom gazed at her granddaughter and smiled. Junhui was busy watching a YouTube video on her cell phone and hardly noticed her grandmother, but it made Mrs. Yeom happy just to look at her. Her daughter and son-in-law were busy discussing finances, something about installment loans or securities, which went over her head. She just wished the food would arrive quickly so she could focus on eating. It was her birthday, after all. She deserved to enjoy herself.

When the food was served, she concentrated on transferring the meat to her mouth. Her daughter attended to Junhui, while her son-in-law managed the grill. After they clinked beer glasses, her daughter seized the moment to say, "Guess what? Junhui's going to start taekwondo soon."

"Why does a girl need to learn taekwondo?"

"Mom, I can't believe an educated, progressive woman like you would say that! What does being a girl have to do with learning taekwondo? A boy in Junhui's class hit her. She wants to learn taekwondo so she can defend herself from bullies."

She was right. These old-fashioned thoughts were embarrassing. While her son-in-law looked on nervously, her daughter finished her beer. Mrs. Yeom glanced at Junhui and tried to relax her face into a smile.

"Junhui, you want to learn taekwondo?"

"Uh-huh," the girl mumbled, not looking up from the phone.

"So, Mom, there's a great taekwondo school in your neighborhood. Apparently, the master was a backup on the national team. He's young and he's got an amazing teaching philosophy. I read about it on the Dongchon Moms Group."

"What's the Dongchon Moms Group?"

"It's an online community for moms in Dongbu Ichon-dong."

"What's the matter with this master? Shouldn't he move his

school to your neighborhood, then? What's he doing in Cheongpa-dong?"

"He's trying, but the rent's too high here. We can't wait for him to move, so we're sending Junhui to Cheongpa-dong for now. But I need your help."

Suddenly, the tender beef felt tough and hard to chew. Of course, she loved spending time with her granddaughter, but not being able to decide when she'd see Junhui made her feel uneasy.

Her daughter was hoping she'd look after Junhui during the two-hour break between taekwondo and violin lessons, and since the shuttle to the violin lesson was unreliable, she wanted Mrs. Yeom to take Junhui there by bus. For a retired grandmother, looking after a grandchild for a few hours shouldn't be difficult, but Mrs. Yeom had her own commitments. She needed to check on the store, volunteer at her church, and transcribe English words daily to stave off dementia. When it came down to it, though, anything concerning her daughter or granddaughter took precedence. Of course it did.

In the end, Mrs. Yeom agreed—as her daughter had known she would. There was no mention of compensation, but she trusted her son-in-law and her daughter to handle everything.

On the bus on her way back from the restaurant, Mrs. Yeom thought of her store staff. She felt at ease around them, and they seemed more like family these days, much more than her rebellious son and ambitious daughter. If she voiced any of this, her daughter would say it was bad business practice to treat one's employees like family, but this was how she felt. She wasn't asking her employees to consider her as family, nor was she making unreasonable demands, as one might with family. Mrs. Yeom only felt this way because she relied on her staff more than anyone else.

Mrs. Oh, who looked after Always Convenience in the morning, was a friend and neighbor she'd known for the past twenty years, as well as a fellow Christian. Hadn't she always treated Mrs. Yeom like a big sister, sharing with her the joys and sorrows of life? And there was Sihyeon, who worked afternoons. She was like a daughter to Mrs. Yeom, which made her want to look out for the girl. Not once had she caused any headaches, other than making the occasional calculation error. Besides, Mrs. Yeom felt completely indebted to the girl for staying put for almost a year, given the high turnover of part-timers. In that regard, Seongpil, who'd worked the graveyard shift for ages, was as dependable as they come. He'd been a godsend, falling straight in her lap a year and a half ago, when Mrs. Yeom had been having trouble replacing the overnight workers who kept quitting. In his mid-fifties, the father of two children lived in a nearby semibasement. He had been a regular, always coming in to buy cigarettes, but as soon as Mrs. Yeom posted a HELP WANTED sign for the night shift, he'd asked if he could apply. Unemployed at the time, he'd been struggling to find work and said with conviction that he needed to contribute somehow. Sensing his desperation, Mrs. Yeom had added an extra 500 won to his minimum wage, which the government had recently increased. And so he was able to take home a monthly salary of over 2 million won. Since then, he'd been working the dreaded graveyard shift.

This is what she meant by family. As a business owner, she hoped they would keep working for her. However, if Sihyeon and Seongpil found proper full-time work and were given the opportunity to achieve their dreams, she planned to send them off happily. Once, she'd even referred Sihyeon for a good job, though the girl had come back right away, unable to last a full day. She vividly recalled Sihyeon asking for her old job back, saying, "I don't think I'm ready to work at an office."

University students worked weekends, and those from the young-adult group at her church covered odd shifts during the week. Now that she had a pool of part-timers who wanted to work just a few days a week for pocket money, Mrs. Yeom didn't need to fill as many shifts herself, and it gave her a break from the constant challenge of finding workers. She remained amazed and grateful whenever her staff called her "Boss" and took care of the store.

There was just one problem—business wasn't great.

Mrs. Yeom could manage on her teacher's pension, but she had decided to run a convenience store on the advice of her younger brother, when she'd been considering what to do with the money her husband had left her. Her brother, who owned three convenience stores, insisted she had to expand to at least three stores to be profitable, but for Mrs. Yeom, managing one was enough. As long as she could live on her pension and her employees could earn a living, that was enough for her. She hadn't anticipated this outcome, but now Mrs. Oh and Seongpil depended on the store for their livelihood. Plus, Sihyeon needed this job while she prepared to take the civil service exam. Thus, Mrs. Yeom, who'd never owned a business or been self-employed, couldn't help but worry about the store when she realized its importance not just for her, but for her entire staff.

Initially, business had been very good, but six months later, two different convenience stores opened within a hundred yards of Always Convenience, leading to fierce competition. As these stores staged aggressive events and promotions, trying to outsell each other, Mrs. Yeom's store experienced a sharp decline in sales. This was where she now found herself.

Mrs. Yeom wasn't trying to make a fortune. Her biggest worry was that her employees would be out of work if her store closed. She hadn't foreseen such intense competition when she started the business, and in all honesty, she didn't know how much longer she could stay open. These were her daily worries, but for now, there wasn't much she could do.

The next day, Mrs. Yeom stopped by the store at eight o'clock in the evening and found the homeless man cleaning the table outside. Hunched over in the autumn chill, he was picking up cigarette butts, paper cups, and empty beer cans from the ground. Though he moved sluggishly, he took the trash to the bins and examined each item before disposing of it in the appropriate bin. Just then, Sihyeon stepped out of the store with a lunch box, placed it on the table, and gestured to him. He acknowledged her with a sloppy bow. She bowed as well and, as she turned to go back inside, noticed Mrs. Yeom.

"Oh, Boss!"

"Bringing him a lunch box, I see?"

"Well, it's the least I can do, since he helps with the cleaning and all . . ."

Sihyeon grinned and went back inside, and Mrs. Yeom turned her attention back to the homeless man. This time, he saw her and bowed, then opened the lid of the lunch box. Without a word, she sat across from him. Steam rose from the lunch box, as if it had been heated in the microwave. He seemed uncomfortable with her sitting there. When she gestured for him to go ahead and eat, he tore the paper wrapper off the chopsticks and took a green glass bottle from his jacket pocket.

He unscrewed the cap from the soju bottle and poured the alcohol into a paper cup he hadn't thrown away. Mrs. Yeom sat across from him in companionable silence, and eventually he seemed to relax, focusing on his meal instead of her presence.

When he was nearly finished, she went into the store and came out with two cups of coffee. She took her seat again and handed him a cup, much to his surprise. With his head bowed, he drank it as if it were honey. Mrs. Yeom sipped hers too. The warm coffee seemed to melt away the bleakness of the weather. In the summer months, residents complained about customers smoking or being too loud while having a beer, and it was difficult to keep the area clean. Despite the complaints, though, she couldn't bring herself to get rid of the patio table—one of the few places where people could sit and take a break.

"It's cold . . . isn't it?"

She looked at the man in shock, as if a ghost had spoken to her. Since he hadn't said a word while eating, she'd assumed he wasn't one for conversation and hadn't asked his name. But now that he'd spoken first, she felt her curiosity rising.

"It sure is. Are you planning to stay at Seoul Station?"

"I sh-should . . . since it'll get colder."

He seemed much more at ease than before. Perhaps coming to the store for lunch boxes had forced him to socialize more. She decided to use this opportunity to ask as many questions as she could.

"Is this the only thing you eat all day?"

"The church service . . . gives you lunch . . . but they m-make you sing hymns . . . I don't like that."

"Well, I wouldn't like that either. Where did you used to live? Have you thought about going back?"

"I . . . don't know."

"Then can I at least have your name?"

"I don't know."

"You mean you don't know your own name? What do people call you? What did you used to do?"

"I don't know."

"Hmm."

At least he was speaking. But why wouldn't he answer her questions? Mrs. Yeom, usually very perceptive, couldn't tell if he genuinely didn't know his name or was just pretending. Still, she decided to press on. To communicate, she needed to know a name to use, at least.

"Then what should I call you?"

Instead of answering, he looked toward Seoul Station. Did he want to go back there, to a familiar place? He then turned and looked her in the eyes.

"Dok . . . go . . ."

"Dokgo?"

"Dokgo . . . Everyone . . . calls me that."

"Is Dokgo your last name or first name?"

"Just . . . Dokgo."

She heaved a sigh and nodded. "Fine, Mr. Dokgo. Don't forget to come here every day. I heard you were late a few days ago. Sihyeon was worried about you."

"There's n-no need . . . to worry."

"When someone who always shows up at the same time is late, of course you worry. So come every day and don't be late. Have a meal and maybe help with the cleaning like today."

"If you lose your w-wallet again . . . let me know."

"Pardon?"

"I'll find it for you. Since I have . . . no way to repay you . . ."

"Are you saying you want me to lose my wallet again so that I can get your help? I thought you were a man of principle." She was teasing him, but he responded earnestly.

"No, no . . . don't lose it . . . Whatever you need . . . just let me know."

Mrs. Yeom felt both pleased and depressed. Did Always Convenience seem so desperate that he thought she needed help, especially from someone like him? Or was he just trying to be kind? Either way, it was time to end the conversation. She looked pointedly at the soju bottle.

"Mr. Dokgo, maybe you should worry about helping yourself first."

He bowed his head, dejected. The poor man was crushed so easily.

"The reason I'm offering you a meal is because I want to help you, even if it's a small gesture, but I can't let you drink here."

He was silent.

"The lunch box isn't a snack to have with your drink. It's a meal. I won't help you get drunk."

"One bottle . . . isn't enough to do anything."

"It doesn't matter. I have rules. This patio table belongs to me, and I can't have you drink here."

He swallowed silently, then gazed at the soju bottle and picked it up. For a second, she wondered if he might attack her with it. But he laid it on top of the empty lunch box container, got up, and trudged to the garbage and recycling bins.

Quietly, she breathed a sigh of relief. He came back to the table, took out a ball of tissue from his jacket, wiped the surface, and bowed to her once more. Mrs. Yeom watched him walk away. Dokgo. Did it mean *godok*, as in *lonely*? Or was he called Dokgo because he lived alone? She told herself that for the time being, she wouldn't let herself worry about that lonesome figure.

"*I'm really sorry*, Boss, but I have to quit before the end of the week," Seongpil said, as soon as he arrived at the store for his overnight shift.

Mrs. Yeom was shocked. Running his hand through what was left of his thinning hair, Seongpil explained he'd found work through an acquaintance as a driver for a small business. Since the new job started in three days, he had to quit the store as soon as possible.

Then, with an apologetic look on his good-natured face, he asked for Mrs. Yeom's understanding.

Replacing him wouldn't be easy—not many people wanted to work nights. Thanks to Seongpil, she'd had peace of mind each night for the past year and a half, but that was about to change. Even if she found someone, the high turnover meant she'd always be looking for replacements. Mrs. Yeom's head was already pounding thinking of her life for the next little while, at least until she found a permanent solution.

She tried to swallow her disappointment, reminding herself of her plan to be happy for Seongpil when he left for another job. She thanked him, telling him how much peace of mind he had given her over the past while, and even mentioned she'd give him a small bonus. Looking visibly moved, he promised to give his best for the last three days.

"You're honestly so cool," Sihyeon said, giving Mrs. Yeom a thumbs-up, as Seongpil went to the back to change into his uniform vest.

"That goes for you, too, Sihyeon. Just focus on passing your government exam. If you pass, I'll buy you a nice work outfit, so study hard."

"Are you serious? Can I get something expensive?"

"Don't you know it'll make a bad impression if a new hire shows up in expensive clothes? I'll buy you something decent. Just study hard."

"All right, Boss."

"Anyway, I need to find someone for the night shift right away. You must have some friends who aren't working full time. Can you ask if any of them would be willing to fill in? I'll also check with the young-adult group at my church."

"Will I get commission if I find someone?"

"Sure. But if you don't, you'll be the one working nights."

"Please, no!"

"If we can't find someone in three days, either you or I will have to fill in. Mrs. Oh can't because of her son, so who else is there? But do you think this granny can work in the middle of the night and stock all the items?" She chuckled.

Sihyeon rolled her eyes at Mrs. Yeom's dramatics.

"I'll try to find someone. I know lots of kids who aren't working right now."

"Tell them what an amazing boss I am."

Smiling, Sihyeon rolled her eyes one last time before getting back to work.

Mrs. Yeom heaved a sigh as she watched countless boxes pour out of the truck. Why had she ordered so many products when business wasn't great? Frustrated with herself, she began to move the boxes that were piling up. At midnight, the delivery person dropped off the products in front of the door, and from there, it was the store's responsibility to move them to the storeroom. Her legs trembled after carrying a few boxes to the back. She sighed again, watching the delivery man put the last boxes on top of the stack and leave.

Almost a week had passed since Seongpil left, but she still hadn't found a replacement for the night shift. For the first three days, a young man from her church filled in. She knew he wasn't a permanent solution, since he was planning to enlist in the army in a few months, but he quit almost immediately, saying his parents disapproved of him working at a convenience store. The little rascal. She wondered how he would manage in the army with that attitude, but right now, she couldn't afford to worry about him.

For the past three days, Mrs. Yeom herself had been covering the night shifts. Sihyeon had begged off with profuse apologies, saying she needed to attend a special "last-minute" lecture early in the morning in Noryangjin. Sly girl! Mrs. Yeom was almost tempted to give Sihyeon a pop quiz. As a former history teacher, she could have helped the girl. But Sihyeon said she preferred to keep Mrs. Yeom as a boss, not a teacher, and politely declined her offers. It occurred to Mrs. Yeom that Sihyeon might be wasting her time working at the store when she should be studying full time.

Mrs. Yeom was doing it again—letting herself get distracted by other people's problems. She needed to focus on her own. She had called her son earlier that day, hoping he might fill in for the night shift, but the conversation ended with her losing her temper. The fool had: 1) asked if she saw him as a deadbeat with nothing better to do; 2) stated that he, with his credentials, was overqualified to work at a convenience store; 3) recommended she just sell the store; and 4) proposed she invest in his new business and take it easy. Far from putting out the fire, the ill-advised phone call had only fanned the flames. After telling him he wouldn't be getting so much as a pack of gum from her store, she hung up. Then she drank a can of beer and crashed, only to be woken by the late-night alarm, reminding her to go to the store to relieve Sihyeon from her shift. Her good-for-nothing son was driving her to drink. Was it okay for a devout woman to act this way? Why would God burden her with her son and a problem, and then give her alcohol, if He didn't want her to drink? She didn't understand.

By the time she moved all the boxes to the back and checked the inventory against the order list, it was past midnight. Now she had to display the new products. For three more hours, she shuffled between the storeroom, shelves, and cooler, like a squirrel carrying acorns. When she finally finished, it was four in the morning. She yawned, leaning against the counter, struggling to keep her eyes open.

Fortunately, there were no customers; she would have been in big trouble otherwise. But feeling relieved there were no customers—if that wasn't a sign the store was in trouble, what was?

Just then, the chime sounded as a group of young people entered, cursing loudly. There were two girls and two boys in their early twenties, visibly drunk. The girls, one with bleached blond hair and the other with purple hair, jabbered away, swearing constantly, while the boys swaggered next to them. Mrs. Yeom was certain the girls weren't from the university. They'd probably wandered into the area after drinking at a bar near Namyeong Station.

"Ah fuck, they don't have Samanco ice waffles here!"

"No, they do. The rice cake ones!"

"I fucking hate those!"

"Then go find ones without rice cakes, stupid. I'm gonna have a B-B-Big!"

"You guys know what Samanco means? *Sa*, as in fucking cheap, and *manco*, as in you get a shitload!"

"You still looking for your dumb Samanco? Christ, where are all the B-B-Bigs? I'm craving red bean."

Mrs. Yeom grimaced as she listened. *Bite your tongue. Even if you say something, these delinquents won't listen anyway.*

"Oh, they have Babambar! Just eat this!"

"Are you stupid? Babambar is chestnut. I said I wanted red bean!"

"Then how about some shaved ice? It's right here!"

"You expect me to eat shaved ice when it's fucking cold out, you shithead?"

"What did you call me? You fu—"

"Students! Stop right there!" Mrs. Yeom yelled, losing her patience.

She told them to mind their language, quickly pay for their items, and head straight home. Never one to tolerate foul language in young people, she couldn't bear their vulgarity another second.

However, she'd made a mistake—they weren't her students. Neither were they well-behaved teens. The four of them advanced, turning feral before her eyes.

The girl with blond hair sidled up to the counter and spat on the floor.

"Hey, Granny, you a cat or something? How many lives you think you got?"

"You're causing trouble. I have it all on camera," Mrs. Yeom warned, trying to stay composed.

The girl with purple hair slammed her ice waffle onto the counter. "Ring it up, or your face is next."

The girls cackled, looking ready to lunge at Mrs. Yeom. The two boys snickered from behind them. Suddenly, anger surged through her.

"You know what? I'm not selling them to you. Get out. If you don't leave right now, I'm calling the police."

The blond girl picked up a Samanco and tapped Mrs. Yeom's head with it. Mrs. Yeom was so shocked her eyes widened. She didn't know what to do.

"Granny, remember what you called us earlier? Students? Do we look like students to you? I swear, old people think every young person is a student. Well, guess what? I don't go to school. I got expelled after beating the shit out of an old teacher like you."

The blond girl was about to tap Mrs. Yeom's cheek with the ice waffle again when Mrs. Yeom grabbed her wrist.

"You really want to get in trouble, don't you?" said Mrs. Yeom.

She squeezed the girl's wrist with all her might. The girl screamed and struggled to break free, but Mrs. Yeom's grip was deceptively strong for a woman her age. When Mrs. Yeom finally let go, the girl lost her balance and fell back, crashing onto the floor. The girl with purple hair grabbed Mrs. Yeom by the shoulder. Without thinking,

Mrs. Yeom seized the girl's hair and yanked her head down onto the counter next to the ice cream.

"What did you say again? You're going to smash my face in? Is that how you talk to your elders?"

The girl struggled frantically, but Mrs. Yeom gave her head a few good shakes before letting go. The girl was breathless and stunned. Seeing the boys' faces harden, Mrs. Yeom hurriedly took the phone off the hook. If the landline phone stayed off the hook for some time, it automatically alerted the closest police station.

"You old bitch! Do you really want to die?"

One of the boys charged toward the cash register, as if he meant to smash it to pieces. Mrs. Yeom shrank back in shock. The boy grinned as he picked up the receiver and placed it back on the cradle.

"You think we've never worked at a convenience store before? Why'd you take it off the hook? You trying to call the police?"

Another mistake. She should have pressed the emergency button on the cash register instead. The boy saw the fear in her eyes and called out to the others.

"Get her! Just take the video footage. And the money!"

She felt her spine grow cold. She couldn't move. The boys began to shout in excitement, and the girls dashed to the register. Mrs. Yeom was terrified. She stood frozen, her hands shaking.

At that second, the chime sounded as the door was flung open.

"You . . . you bastards!" a voice thundered.

The teens' heads spun around, and there was Dokgo's towering frame filling the doorway. She couldn't believe her eyes.

"How dare you . . . treat your elders this way!" he roared.

This intimidating figure looked nothing like the mumbling and sluggish homeless man she had met at Seoul Station. Mrs. Yeom stared in awe, as if an army had come to her rescue. However, the delinquents didn't seem to see Dokgo the same way.

"What the fuck? Ah, what's that smell?"

"I think he's homeless. Fucking nasty. Jesus Christ!"

The boys rushed toward Dokgo, but he stood his ground, withstanding the attacks. He took the beatings with his whole body while blocking the door. When Dokgo continued to shield his face, the boys' punches grew more aggressive, until he curled up in a ball in front of the door and remained motionless. She couldn't help him, so she did the only thing she could and pushed the emergency button.

Almost immediately, however, she heard the wail of a siren growing closer. The girls noticed it first, and the boys looked startled. They tried to push Dokgo aside and flee, but he wouldn't budge, blocking the door with his hulking figure.

"Fucking move! Move, you piece of shit!"

The boys stopped struggling when two men in uniform appeared. Only then was Mrs. Yeom able to calm her racing heart. She saw Dokgo's broad back as he slowly got up to open the door for the police officers. Suddenly, he turned and offered her an expression that was half grin, half grimace, his face covered with blood. It was the first time she was seeing him smile. He didn't seem bothered by the blood at all.

At the police station, the father of one of the teenagers arrived. The middle-aged man took one look at Dokgo's swollen, bloody face and proposed a settlement. Surprisingly, Dokgo requested something other than money. He walked up to the four teens, who still seemed drunk, and ordered them to kneel and face the corner with their hands raised above their heads. They hesitated at first, but when the father yelled at them, they obeyed, looking like elementary school students being punished.

After leaving the police station, Mrs. Yeom and Dokgo walked to the early-morning market. They passed merchants preparing for the day and headed to a hangover soup joint down a side street. With Band-Aids covering his face, Dokgo shoveled seonji soup into his mouth, while she barely touched her food, overwhelmed with worry and frustration.

"Kids these days are scary. What were you thinking, challenging them like that?" she asked.

"I told you . . . I can handle two . . ."

He touched the Band-Aids as if they were badges of honor and smiled, showing his teeth. Mrs. Yeom was about to continue when she realized she had challenged those same kids herself. She gave a bitter smile and studied him.

"Thank you," she finally said.

"So I earned . . . my meal?"

"Of course. But how did you know to show up right then?"

"I heard you were working nights . . . I couldn't sleep . . . got worried . . . so I came."

"Hmm. I'm more worried about you, actually."

Embarrassed, he scratched his head and spooned more soup into his mouth.

"You walked in so confidently, I thought you must've been in a few fights in your youth. But I didn't expect you to just take a beating. Thank goodness that patrol car showed up when it did, or you could have been seriously hurt."

"I . . . called them."

"What?"

"There's a p-pay phone there . . . I saw the kids causing trouble . . . so I called the police and walked in . . . I knew if I let them hit me for a bit . . . the police would come . . ."

Mrs. Yeom's mouth dropped open. He wasn't just a man of principle. He was smart too. But more importantly, he had watched over her store and even taken blows on her behalf. She was suddenly overcome with admiration and gratitude. She looked at Dokgo, who had gone back to eating and scratching his head.

"Do you want some soju?"

His swollen eyes widened. "Really?"

"But this will be your last. Come work at the store, but on one condition: you have to quit drinking."

"M-me?" Dokgo asked, tilting his large head to the side.

"I know you can do it. It'll get colder soon, but you can stay warm and make some money."

She stared into his eyes, waiting for his answer. Dokgo looked away, his face twitching, as if caught in a dilemma. Finally, he lifted his small eyes to meet hers.

"Why are you . . . so nice to me?"

"I'm just doing what you did for me. Besides, I can't work nights anymore. It's too hard, and I get scared. You've got to do it."

"But . . . you don't . . . know me."

"I do know. You're someone who helps me."

"I don't even know myself . . . How can you trust me?"

"I've met thousands of students in my previous career. I've learned to be a good judge of character. If you stop drinking, you'll be fine."

For some time, Dokgo stroked his beard and bit his lips. Asking him to work for her had been impulsive, but she already knew she'd be disappointed if he said no. She fought the urge to tell him to stop fiddling with his beard and just answer already.

At last, he looked at her as if he'd made a decision.

"One more bottle then . . . Quitting after one bottle is kind of unfair . . ."

"Fine, two bottles. After we finish here, I'll give you some money.

Go to the bathhouse, clean yourself up, get a haircut, and buy some new clothes, okay? Then come to the store tonight."

"Th-thank you."

Mrs. Yeom ordered two bottles. She twisted off the cap, poured him a shot, and poured herself one too. They sealed the employment contract with a toast.

2

The Biggest PIA of Them All

It seemed only natural that Sihyeon's final stop in her long sequence of part-time jobs would be at a convenience store. Not only was she a frequent convenience store customer, but she also discovered that the abilities acquired at her previous part-time jobs were easily transferable. The customer service and cashier skills she honed at the cosmetics store were almost identical to those needed at the convenience store, and her experience of sorting parcels at a courier company proved useful in managing merchandise. At the franchise coffee shop, she had learned to deal with difficult customers, internally referred to as PIAs: pains in the ass. This was further strengthened at a Korean BBQ restaurant, where she developed an even thicker skin by dealing with PIAs who blamed the staff for overcooking their meat when the customers themselves had grilled it.

The convenience store was where all these tasks, scenarios, and PIAs came together. Sihyeon started working at the store a year ago, completing her training in half a day. Since then, she has worked eight hours a day, from 2:00 p.m. to 10:00 p.m., while preparing to take her civil service exam. The main reason she has lasted this long was the store owner, who was a decent human being. The boss is the most important factor in determining how long part-timers stay, and the owner, a retired high school history teacher, represented the kind of adult Sihyeon thought she could truly respect. These days, to avoid giving paid leave, convenience stores don't schedule their staff for five days a week. Instead, workers are offered only two or three days, making it impossible to live on just one job. But Sihyeon's boss scheduled all her regular staff for five days a week. She was also clear about what they needed to do, as opposed to what she needed to do. She led by example and, most importantly, treated the employees with respect.

"Value your workers, and they'll value the customers." This was something Sihyeon grew up hearing from her parents, who were veterans in the restaurant business. Ultimately, a store is about people. A store that fails to value its customers, much like a boss who fails to value their employees, is destined for the same outcome: failure. In this respect, the Cheongpa-dong convenience store was unlikely to fail. However, making money remained challenging. Recently, two other convenience stores had opened nearby, and in this neighborhood, with its large elderly population, local marts were preferred over convenience stores. The store's saving grace was its proximity to Sookmyung Women's University, but even this didn't offer much help, since Always Convenience was tucked away slightly off the main road. Only those students renting rooms in the neighborhood regularly frequented the store.

Business being slow made work easier for Sihyeon. How could she leave a job that offered so much to its staff? However, she couldn't help wanting to drum up more business for the owner, so she tried her best to serve each customer with care, hoping to attract regulars.

And yet, despite all her skills and training, there was one PIA she couldn't stand. He was a recent regular, probably in his mid-forties and new to the area, skinny with bulging eyes and a foul temper. From his first visit, he had startled her with his rudeness, always tossing money onto the counter. He was condescending, barking commands and expecting immediate compliance as if she were a machine. He often pointed out her mistakes, allowing her no chance to rectify them and only adding to her frustration and resentment. Once, he turned up at the counter with the buy-two-get-one snacks a day after the promotion ended, and when the discount wasn't applied at checkout, anger flashed in his eyes.

"Where's my discount?"

"Sir, this promotion ended yesterday. I'm afraid the discount can't be applied."

"Then why didn't you take down the sign? I picked these out specifically for the discount. How are you going to compensate me for the time I wasted? I demand a discount."

"Sorry, but I can't do that. The promo period is written clearly on the sign. If you had checked—"

"I don't have my reading glasses with me, so how am I supposed to read the tiny print? It's hard for anyone over forty. Are you ageist? As an apology, give me the discount now."

"I'm sorry, but I can't do that."

"Then forget the lousy snacks. I don't want them anyway. Just give me my cigarettes."

"Which kind would you like?"

"The same kind I always get. I buy my cigarettes here every day. If this is how you treat your regulars, no wonder business here sucks. Christ."

Her first mistake was failing to remove the old promotion sign, and her second was losing her composure and asking him which cigarettes he wanted, even though she knew what he always got. To be fair, the first situation could have been avoided if he had brought his reading glasses, and the second was hardly a mistake. But the PIA used it all as an excuse to make Sihyeon's life a living hell.

After getting his cigarettes and hurling his money on the counter, he collected his change and sat at the patio table to smoke. Ignoring the No Smoking sign, he flicked his cigarette butt on the ground. Always keen to point out the slightest faults in others but never willing to reflect on his own, this PIA was truly the worst.

Between 8:00 and 9:00 p.m., whenever it was time for this PIA to show up, Sihyeon would start to feel anxious. And from the moment the door chimed and he entered with his bulging, goldfish eyes, her heart pounded until he paid for his things and left. She couldn't help feeling nervous, as she wondered what trouble he'd cause that day. She told herself that all she had to do was make it past the hour when he came to get his cigarettes and snacks.

One evening in late autumn, when Mrs. Yeom walked into the store with a man, Sihyeon was so shocked her mouth dropped open. For the first time, she realized just how much facial hair—or the lack of it—could drastically alter a man's appearance. Sure, she knew what a nice haircut could do for a person, but the moment she saw Dokgo, with his usual unkempt, weed-like mustache and beard neatly trimmed, she couldn't help but think he looked like a respectable uncle, not the homeless man she'd tried to avoid. With a fresh haircut and dressed in a loose shirt and jeans instead of his dirty windbreaker and trousers, he looked like a completely different person. Though his eyes were small, she couldn't deny that the high bridge of his nose, his well-groomed facial hair, and his strong jawline exuded masculinity. On top of that, his broad shoulders and back made him seem dependable, and now that he stood straight and confident instead of hunched over, he even looked taller.

Dusting an invisible speck from his shoulder and presenting

Dokgo as if he were a son who had just won a major prize, Mrs. Yeom announced that he would be covering the night shift from now on. The boss couldn't be serious! Although Sihyeon was impressed by Dokgo's transformation, her heart sank at the suggestion that she take on the responsibility of training him. But what choice did she have? She had to follow the boss's orders.

Sihyeon suggested that Mrs. Yeom, with her extensive teaching experience, would be better suited, but Mrs. Yeom wouldn't hear of it. She argued that young Sihyeon had a better grasp of the point-of-sale system and customer service, and as a compromise, Mrs. Yeom would take charge of training him on receiving midnight deliveries and managing merchandise displays. Sihyeon reluctantly agreed. Together, they would bring Dokgo up to speed. After all, Mrs. Yeom couldn't cover the night shift forever.

To be honest, Sihyeon wasn't particularly dependable or meticulous. More of a loner, she didn't have many friends. After college, she had decided to prepare for the entry-level civil service exam only because the monotonous nature of that kind of job seemed to suit her personality. The problem was that everyone around her had the same idea. Lured by the promise of job security, her peers with stronger résumés and diverse experiences were also preparing for the exam, driving up the competition. She thought, *You're popular and outgoing, and you studied abroad. Why are you settling for a dull civil servant job when you could go for something more exciting? Shouldn't you leave these boring jobs for ordinary people like me?*

Meanwhile, Mrs. Yeom's convenience store gave Sihyeon a glimpse of civil service life. Her routine included attending morning classes in Noryangjin, working at the store from afternoon to evening, and then returning to her home in Sadang-dong. Her mother didn't understand why she had to travel all the way to Cheongpa-dong when there were closer stores, but to Sihyeon, there was nothing more humiliating than running into people she knew while working at a neighborhood convenience store. Plus, a past crush had lived in this neighborhood. She'd met him here a couple of times, and so Cheongpa-dong held special memories for her. They'd even had a semidate at the Waffle House, sharing a delicious strawberry shaved ice. He had abruptly gone on a working holiday to Australia and hadn't returned in years. For all she knew, he had settled down with a tall Australian woman or fallen in love with feeding baby kangaroos.

Anyhow, the convenience store on the corner of a Cheongpa-dong side street has become her sanctuary. She has no intention of leaving until she passes her civil service exam. Especially after her dream of taking a working holiday in Japan fell through, she became even more determined to stay. Japan had seemed an obvious choice—she was a Japanese-language graduate and anime fan—but the trade war between Japan and Korea that began in June made her plans impossible. Even her dream of traveling to small Japanese towns on weekends and holidays once she became a civil servant was shattered.

Seeing her personal dreams crumble due to diplomatic issues made Sihyeon realize she was part of society after all. She had believed she was different from those who cheered for soccer games or gathered in public squares to protest with candlelight. Her world existed within a computer monitor in the corner of her room. With just Netflix and the internet, she had everything she needed to access the world and enjoy life, and she found peace in her personal refuge—the convenience store. Sometimes, she wondered if, deep down, she secretly wanted to work at the store forever and forget about the civil service exam. After all, wasn't working for the government just like working at a larger convenience store? Wasn't that a life where she would deal with bigger PIAs while serving the public? . . . This place was her haven, and she needed to protect it.

What this all meant was that she needed to help with Dokgo's transformation. She'd been happy to give him expired lunch boxes, but training and talking to him was a different story. First, she had to get used to his stuttering and sluggish movements. But more than anything, she had to put up with the lingering smell of homelessness that clung to him, no matter how much he showered.

Dokgo worked hard to absorb everything Sihyeon said, taking notes in an old notebook, wiping off the excess ink from his pen, and diligently writing down the proper way to greet customers. He even noted the rules for merchandise display, supplementing them with sketches. Touched by his effort, Sihyeon patiently instructed him. When customers arrived, she nudged the hesitant Dokgo with her elbow, prompting him to greet them. He would then mumble, "Wel-wel . . . come," but customers never replied, mistaking his shy greetings as part of his conversation with Sihyeon. Sighing, she led him to the cash register, demonstrating the checkout process while he stood beside her. However, he was far from ready to manage the register alone.

"The boss will stay with you tonight, but you're on your own starting tomorrow, so make sure you remember everything."

"G-got it. But . . . to scan those two items together . . ."

"Just trust the computer. Everything's already programmed. New products are automatically updated, so all you have to do is point the bar code scanner and scan."

"Just point . . . and scan."

"And what do you scan?"

"Th-the products."

"Which part do you scan?"

"That thing . . . with the lines . . . the bar something?"

"The bar code. Just aim at the bar code lines and scan. Okay?"

"Okay."

Sihyeon felt a flash of annoyance, but she was also proud of herself for teaching a man at least twenty years older than her. But most of all, she was pleased by the approving looks Mrs. Yeom gave her while chatting with a friend at a table inside the store. Sihyeon liked her boss. If she had met a teacher like Mrs. Yeom during her school days, who knows? She might have become a history buff instead of an anime fan.

In any case, she had to get this awkward, inexperienced man, freshly graduated from homelessness, to work the cash register on his own. Trying to tamp down her irritation, Sihyeon shot a sharp glance at Dokgo, who was busy sketching bar codes in his notebook.

The next day, when Sihyeon stepped into the store after her class, Mrs. Oh hurried over to her from the counter.

"Sihyeon, what's with the bumbling fool?"

Sihyeon snickered, finding the outdated term unexpectedly fitting. Mrs. Oh wanted an explanation, as though she believed Sihyeon was responsible for hiring Dokgo. Mrs. Oh always sounded accusatory. Whether it was her nature or the result of dealing with her unruly son, she was aggressive and confrontational, even with customers.

"Were you the one who recommended him? Who the heck is he? He can't do anything right, and he can barely get a word out without stuttering."

"It wasn't me. The boss found him." Not wanting to elaborate further, Sihyeon kept her expression neutral and headed to the storeroom.

Mrs. Oh spoke respectfully only when speaking to the boss, who happened to be her neighbor and a fellow church member. She was very attached to Mrs. Yeom, whom she affectionately called eonni. This made sense, given that Mrs. Oh—despite what she thought of herself—was impatient and hot-tempered, not exactly suited for the service industry. So of course she would be devoted to the boss, who not only accepted her but had also given her a job. As Sihyeon emerged wearing her uniform vest, Mrs. Oh started grumbling again.

"Where on earth did she find him? She didn't say a word to me. Sihyeon, do you know anything? Come on, spit it out."

"I really don't know."

Sihyeon decided not to say anything more. If she mentioned that Dokgo used to be homeless, Mrs. Oh would stay long after her shift, sticking to her like glue and complaining nonstop. Sihyeon sighed. She longed for the day when she'd be able to start her shift without Mrs. Oh's endless chatter and probing questions.

"I don't get it. It seems like she picked just anyone because the night shift's been tough, but I'm telling you, that guy looks like trouble. He'll probably get into fights with drunk customers, mess up the transactions, or maybe he's even planning to rob the store . . . We should let the boss know this is a bad idea."

"I don't know, he doesn't seem like a bad person."

"Who's bad from the start? Sihyeon, you're too naïve to see it, but you really need to watch out for these slow, unassuming types. The boss has only worked in a school, so she has no idea how many bad people are out there."

"He really doesn't seem dangerous. But I had a hard time trying to teach him how to use the cash register, which was frustrating. What can we do though? There's no one to work the night shift right now."

"That's why I'm asking if you have any friends who aren't working right now."

It was a mistake to engage. Mrs. Oh's questions weren't going to stop now.

"I don't have many friends."

"You're young. How can you have no friends? You need to get out more, live a little."

Was she trying to pick a fight? Suppressing a flash of anger, Sihyeon forced a bright smile.

"Mrs. Oh, what about your son? Didn't you recently say you were fed up with him sitting at home playing games all day?"

"My son? He can't work here. He's prepping for the civil service exam these days . . . I don't know why he's even bothering with it. I told him he should try for the foreign service exam instead and become a diplomat. He sure has the brains for it."

Aaaand Mrs. Oh for the victory. It was impossible to win against the woman.

"You know, diplomats are civil servants too," Sihyeon muttered under her breath, as she pretended to be busy with the monitor.

Mrs. Oh went back to griping about the bumbling bear of a man, emphasizing that she was the one who *really* ran the store. *Why is she unloading all of this on me instead of talking to the boss, who could actually do something about it?* It seemed she was jealous of the kind treatment Mrs. Yeom had been showing Sihyeon lately and wanted to put her in her place. But why get competitive? They didn't even work the same shift.

Sihyeon made a decision right then and there: She would pass her civil service exam and say goodbye to the convenience store. She'd leave right after getting the satisfaction of seeing Mrs. Oh's son bomb the foreign service exam.

Mrs. Oh wished her luck and rushed off. Alone at last. Just as Sihyeon let out a sigh of relief, a group of college girls walked in, lighting up the place with their chatter. *Enjoy these years while they last,* Sihyeon thought. *As soon as you graduate, it's job hunting and scraping by on a tiny wage like me.* The thought made her feel older and depressed.

Twenty-seven already, with no special skills, no money, no partner; her youth was slipping away. Thirty was just around the corner, the age she always saw as the end of the good times.

"Hello?"

Sihyeon snapped back to reality. The three students were staring at her, their items spread out on the counter. Pushing worries about her approaching age aside, she focused on ringing up their things.

He arrived for his shift. Winter was approaching, and not only was he lucky enough to spend his nights in a warm store instead of being out in the cold like before, but he also got free meals and a wage—he had truly hit the jackpot. As if he knew this himself, Dokgo rolled in just before eight, looking sharper than ever.

He was supposed to keep shadowing Sihyeon, learning how to greet customers and handle the register, until ten o'clock, when her shift ended. After that, he was to learn the night-shift duties from the boss. Today marked his second day, and who knew how long it would take him to master everything? Sihyeon, who was training him as a favor to Mrs. Yeom, was already feeling her patience wearing thin, and he'd only been here a few minutes. As soon as he entered the store, instead of properly greeting her, he made a beeline for the storeroom. He came out moments later with a packet of instant coffee mix, poured it into a steaming cup of water, and drank it while gazing out the window. And it wasn't just any old coffee mix—it was a Kanu Black! It came from the boss's special stash, which neither Sihyeon nor Mrs. Oh dared to touch. Yet here he was, on his second day on the job, sipping it with elegance as if he were Gong Yoo himself in those Kanu ads . . . It was unreal.

"Got so sleepy . . . at night . . . so I kept drinking coffee. She said . . . this was the best," Dokgo said, having wandered over to Sihyeon at some point.

Sihyeon scoffed and barked, "Kanu Black is only for the boss, because she's diabetic!"

He nodded and mumbled something. Thinking he was cursing under his breath, Sihyeon snapped, "What did you just say?"

"So that's why . . . Boss told me . . . to drink this . . ."

"Excuse me?"

"Diabetes . . . It's common . . . with homeless people . . ."

"What did you say?"

"Our diets are a mess . . . bad kidneys . . ."

"Says who?"

"An expert . . . from a morning program . . . I watch TV at Seoul Station every day . . ."

She grunted in response.

For the second time that day, Sihyeon told herself to bite her tongue. Mrs. Oh talked too much, and Dokgo took forever to say the few things on his mind. Communication with either of them was a headache. She wanted to work with people who understood her. Why was the boss so big on giving people second chances? Was it because she used to be a teacher? Or because she's a deacon at her church? Or did everyone grow more patient with age?

At the sound of the chime, Sihyeon gave Dokgo a look. Again, he muttered a belated "Wel . . . come . . ." He gulped down his coffee and shuffled to the counter. Sihyeon stepped aside, ready to observe him work the register, when it hit her—the man walking in was the PIA! She'd enjoyed a brief respite these last few days without him, as if a painful tooth had been plucked out, but now he was back, and he'd shown up during Dokgo's training.

"It's the PIA," she whispered into Dokgo's ear. "Pay attention."

"The PI . . . what?"

"Pain in the ass. I told you PIA stands for pain in the ass."

"Ah, pain in the ass . . . Where is he?"

"Shh! Keep it down or he'll—"

Before Sihyeon could warn Dokgo, the PIA strolled up to the counter and tossed down a few snack bags. Dokgo clumsily held the bar code scanner, like a monkey trying to use a smartphone, and fumbled with a bag of chips, struggling to find the bar code on the colorful packaging. That was the mistake. He should have asked if the PIA wanted to purchase a bag. *Whatever, let's see how this goes,* Sihyeon thought, deciding to just watch. At last, Dokgo found the bar code, scanned the rest of the items, and stuttered out the total.

The PIA glanced at Sihyeon and grinned. He seemed to have figured out they were in the middle of training. "Cigarettes," he said.

Dokgo looked at the PIA and tilted his head. "I-I don't smoke . . ."

"I didn't mean for you. For me."

"Oh, cigarettes . . . So, what kind?"

"'So, what kind?' How dare you speak to a customer that way? How old are you?"

"I-I don't know."

"You think you're real funny, don't you? Are you stupid or what?"

"Nope . . . So, what do you want?" Dokgo asked, still speaking informally.

The PIA snorted and turned to look at Sihyeon. Sihyeon reached for the cigarette display, but the PIA held up his hand to stop her. Staring at Dokgo, he said, "Let's see if you're as stupid as you look. I want a pack of Esse Change four milligrams. Now!"

Esse was a brand with many varieties, so one needed to be careful. This was especially true for the Esse Change series, which included a wide range: Change, Change Up, Change Linn, Change Bing, Change Himalaya, and so on, which could be extremely confusing. For Sihyeon, who didn't smoke, remembering all the different types of Esse cigarettes that customers requested had been challenging at first. The PIA, who usually smoked Dunhill 6 mg, was purposely asking Dokgo for a difficult one.

Dokgo plucked out the correct pack of Esse cigarettes from the display without any hesitation and scanned the bar code. The PIA, perhaps not wanting to be outdone, tossed his card down this time. Dokgo calmly picked it up, processed the payment, and handed it back to the PIA.

"How about my bag?" the PIA asked, as if quizzing Dokgo.

Sihyeon resisted the urge to intervene. Dokgo looked from the items to the PIA and then grinned.

"Just . . . carry them home. Plastic bags . . . are bad for the environment."

The PIA's face hardened, and he leaned toward Dokgo, as if challenging him.

"I live far from here. How am I supposed to carry everything home without a bag?"

"Then . . . buy one."

"You should have asked me first. You expect me to put that on my card? Just gimme one."

"Sorry . . . c-can't do that."

"You're inconveniencing a customer and refusing to make things right. This is a *convenience* store, isn't it?" he said sarcastically.

At his half-mocking, half-threatening tone, Sihyeon suddenly felt nervous. The situation was going out of control. She was about to step in, but Dokgo suddenly clapped his hands.

Then, to the amazement of both Sihyeon and the PIA, Dokgo went into the storeroom and came back with his own reusable bag, an old, dingy canvas bag stamped with some charity's logo. He dumped its contents on the counter next to the cash register. Pens, a notebook, and recently expired sandwiches tumbled out. Dokgo began putting the PIA's purchases into the empty bag. The PIA scoffed, glaring at Dokgo as if he were an animal.

"What the hell are you doing?"

"Use this . . . to take your things . . ."

"You expect me to put my things in that nasty bag?"

"If you wash it . . . it'll be fine . . ."

Sihyeon couldn't just stand by and watch anymore. "I'm sorry. He's still in training. I'll put your things in a plastic bag."

Sihyeon reached for the reusable bag now filled with the PIA's items. But Dokgo refused to let go of the bag. Ignoring Sihyeon, he stretched out his arm, holding the bag right in front of the PIA's face. The PIA glared at Dokgo for a long time, and Sihyeon looked on helplessly.

Dokgo's small eyes, narrowed to slits, appeared especially cold, and his pursed lips and broad chin jutted out menacingly. He continued to stand there in silence, the bag dangling from his outstretched arm. Not sure what to do, Sihyeon turned to look at the PIA. He was glaring at Dokgo, his goldfish eyes practically popping out of his head. His initial shock quickly became annoyance. He snatched the bag from Dokgo and left the store, holding it away from himself in disgust.

Sihyeon sagged with relief now that the standoff between the two men was over. Meanwhile, as if nothing had happened, Dokgo simply went back to writing in his notebook. "Always ask if they'd like a bag first . . ." Sihyeon cleared her throat, trying to shake off the memory of how intimidating Dokgo had looked.

"Anyway, it was good you didn't give him the bag."

"I-I'm sorry. I . . . forgot. You . . . told me to ask . . ."

"There's no need to be sorry. Just don't forget next time. And even though he's a PIA, you can't fight with customers."

"I can handle two . . . no problem."

She didn't know if he meant fighting two people or handling two customers at once, but his grinning face showed no trace of the intimidating figure she'd just seen. Sighing, she remembered what she'd been curious about.

"Anyway, how did you manage to find the cigarettes so quickly?"

"Last night . . . so many customers were buying cigarettes . . . I decided to just memorize them all. For Esse, there's Esse One, Esse Special Gold, Esse Special Gold 1 mg, Esse Special Gold 0.5, Esse Classic, Esse Soo 0.5, Esse Soo 0.1, Esse Golden Leaf, Esse Golden Leaf 1 mg . . ."

He recited them like the multiplication tables. Stunned, Sihyeon said nothing for a while before finally interrupting, "How did you memorize all that in one day?"

"I had nothing to do during the night . . . and I kept getting sleepy . . ."

"Were you a smoker before?"

"I-I don't know."

"You don't know if you used to smoke?"

"I can't remember."

"Do you have amnesia?"

"My head got messed up . . . from drinking."

"Then what can you remember?"

"I don't know."

Jeez . . . Sihyeon regretted forgetting her earlier resolve to stay quiet. Despite her discomfort, she had to admit it was satisfying to see the PIA put in his place. Sihyeon decided not to hold a grudge against Dokgo for drinking the Kanu coffee. Even though her shift was almost over, the boss still hadn't shown up. Sihyeon texted her and got a response: I went to the Wednesday service and got home now. Starting tonight, Dokgo will work alone. Sihyeon texted: You think he's ready? and Mrs. Yeom replied: What do you think?

Hmm . . . Sihyeon started to text. Thinking, Sihyeon observed Dokgo stock the shelf with Buldak Hot Chicken Ramen, muttering the different varieties to himself: "Nuclear Buldak, Cheese Buldak, Carbo . . . nara Buldak . . ." She watched him squat down and mumble to himself while carefully lining up the noodle bowls with his hands. She texted the boss: Yes.

A week passed. Dokgo arrived at eight o'clock sharp every night, always in the same outfit and with the same shuffling steps, but he had shed the "fool" part of his nickname. Though his actions were still slow, his stuttering had lessened, and he diligently carried out his tasks: cleaning both the outdoor and indoor tables, restocking empty shelves, taking the expired goods off the shelves, and even wiping down the walk-in cooler with a rag without being asked.

He no longer needed any training. There was nothing more for Sihyeon to teach him. He managed well on his own, which only prompted her to become more curious about him. Even though it was time for the evening rush, the store was unusually quiet, and Sihyeon and Dokgo stood at the counter, eating gimbap with milk.

"Where do you stay during the day, mister?" Sihyeon asked, finishing her strawberry milk.

He hurriedly swallowed his bite of gimbap and turned to her. "The boss . . . gave me an advance . . . Got a small room . . . in Dongja-dong . . . across from Seoul Station . . ."

"So you sleep there during the day and come here in the evening? Do you cook your meals there?"

"The room . . . is like a coffin . . . Once you lie down . . . that's it . . . After work, I eat the expired sandwiches on my way home . . . I sleep . . . then go to Seoul Station to watch TV and come here."

"Do you have to go to Seoul Station? What if you bump into your old buddies and get pulled back into that life?"

"That won't happen . . . Seoul Station is . . . where I watch TV . . . and people . . ."

"Your stutter's almost gone now. Does that mean your memory's coming back too? Are you starting to remember your home, family, your old job, and stuff like that?"

Dokgo paused for a moment, then shook his head. Then he stuffed the last two gimbap pieces into his mouth, picked up the milk carton, and sucked on the straw. Sihyeon watched him lick his lips after finishing the milk and asked, "It's not bad working here, right?"

"Everything's good . . . except that I can't drink."

"Mister, you have a job, a place to sleep, and free food on top of that, so you shouldn't complain about not being able to drink."

"I can get a bed at the center . . . and I can eat for free at soup kitchens . . . But if I work, I can't drink . . . so I get these headaches."

"You're going through withdrawal—I get it. But staying off alcohol will make you feel better soon, okay?

He smiled at Sihyeon, his eyes crinkling until they disappeared. His smile made her proud she'd been able to teach this older man everything she knew.

"You've graduated! The boss said you've learned everything you need to know, so no more coming in at eight. Starting tomorrow, you can come in at ten."

"Thank you. I learned a lot . . . It's all because of you."

"Don't mention it."

"I'm serious . . . You have a knack . . . Everything you said . . . just clicked in my head."

"You sure know how to flatter someone, don't you? You must have done pretty well for yourself in the past. I bet you couldn't stand me when I was telling you what to do."

"No, no . . . My mind's a complete blank . . . totally empty, but you're a great teacher. If you don't believe me . . . post it online. How to use the POS system . . . You're really good at teaching that."

"Where in the world would I post that?"

"On You . . . Yooktube . . ."

"You mean YouTube? Why would I do that?"

"For people who need it . . . I'm sure they do."

"So you're saying I should post a tutorial on how to use the POS system on YouTube?"

"It'll help people. There are so many convenience stores . . . and so many part-timers . . . If you teach it the way you taught me . . ."

"I've got enough on my plate. When I get home, I need to study."

"But you helped me."

"Because the boss told me to."

"I know, but still . . . you're a good teacher."

Right then, Sihyeon had an epiphany. She had genuinely helped this man, and it was something she could take pride in—something she hadn't felt for a long time, not until Dokgo came into her life.

"And that Yook . . . YouTube thing . . . I heard you can make money from it. I saw it on TV."

Dokgo's eyes shone. Normally, she would have laughed, but she soon found herself deep in thought. Then she struggled to recall her YouTube login details, which she hadn't used in a long time.

"Hello, welcome to the second tutorial of 'Learning the Always Convenience Store POS System,'" Sihyeon said into a microphone she had bought online for 26,500 won. She spoke clearly while recording the cash register monitor with her phone.

"Last week, we covered the different parts of the POS system and their basic functions. Today, we're going to explore some of the more advanced features, such as how to process split transactions, handle returns, and top up transit cards. Why don't we start with split transactions? Let's say a customer brings a product to the counter, but they want to pay using both cash and card. Don't panic, just follow these steps."

The camera shifted to show a chocolate bar on the counter.

"First, scan the bar code and check the price. It's thirty-two hundred won. But the customer wants to pay three thousand won in cash and two hundred won by card. Some customers request multiple payment methods so that they can avoid carrying change. Start by entering two hundred won in the POS as the amount received. This is the card payment. Next, insert the credit card and select 'Payment.' This will charge two hundred won to the card. Now, for the remaining three thousand won, receive it in cash and press 'Payment' again. And you're done. Pretty easy, right?"

After pausing the recording to catch her breath, Sihyeon reviewed the content. The video showed only her hands, the POS, and the product, while her clear, calm voice explained the complicated payment process step-by-step. By describing every detail slowly, similar to how she'd taught Dokgo, she aimed to simplify things for those less familiar with the technology. Not being tech savvy herself, she, too, had struggled with the POS system at first. Now, operating it was a breeze, and teaching it through video felt as straightforward as tossing expired lunches. She cleared her throat and resumed filming.

"Let's move on to processing returns. First, click 'Receipts' on the POS..."

The response was unexpectedly positive. Of course, there were other tutorials on YouTube—one that kept cutting between a pretty face and the POS, leaving you unsure if the goal was to teach or to flaunt, and another produced like a game show, full of flashy graphics, subtitles, and music. Compared to those, Sihyeon's videos were simple and plain, almost minimalist, but that aspect appealed to those seeking more practical tutorials. What mattered most was that Sihyeon responded to every question from those new to working in convenience stores.

Viewers appreciated Sihyeon's video for her slow, methodical explanations. She presented the information as if teaching young students, making it easy to digest. Some comments described her low voice as soothing, putting listeners at ease rather than making them feel like they were in a lecture. Sihyeon, curious, tried speaking aloud to herself, amazed that the voice she always found grating had a calming effect on others.

Dokgo continued to arrive an hour early to sweep the floor and tidy the outdoor table before taking over the shift from Sihyeon. He had fully adjusted to the night shift, and it was hard to believe that less than a month ago, he had been a homeless man living at Seoul Station. The thick white jacket he'd purchased with his first paycheck made him look less like a fierce grizzly bear and more like the polar bear from a Coca-Cola ad, and his size made him a rock of dependability for both the boss and Sihyeon. Just the day before, they had managed to quickly assemble and set up the Christmas tree, thanks to his help. Best of all, the nasty PIA hadn't shown his face around the store since his confrontation with Dokgo. It was typical of the PIA to bully those weaker than himself and cower before those stronger. Only Mrs. Oh still seemed bothered by Dokgo. Now, her routine was to complain about him when Sihyeon arrived for her shift. The older woman appeared to have chosen Dokgo as the target for her frustrations. But he didn't seem to care. Once, when Sihyeon asked if Mrs. Oh stressed him out, he shook his head and gave a small smile.

"Stress is . . . that." He pointed to the coolers in the back corner of the store.

"Pardon me?"

"That liquor cooler . . . it's too close . . ."

"You can't start drinking again! Seriously!" Sihyeon cried, raising her voice involuntarily.

As if sensing her embarrassment over the outburst, Dokgo nodded. "Actually, I have . . . a plan," he said with a chuckle.

Sihyeon felt relieved. She now automatically restocked the Kanu coffee mixes Dokgo drank. Helping him had shown her the value in assisting others and made her realize she did have a special talent after all. Just yesterday, while filming her YouTube video, she found herself thinking of him. She moved and spoke in a calm, deliberate manner, as though she were instructing him. Maybe the key to helping people was to approach them more slowly, more patiently? It seemed that she, once an outcast disconnected from society, had finally found a sense of connection.

The day before Christmas Eve, Sihyeon received an unfamiliar email in the inbox linked to her YouTube account. A woman, claiming to run two Always Convenience stores, expressed interest in working with her and left her phone number.

What was this—a scouting offer?

The idea of being scouted as a convenience store worker seemed far-fetched. And if she was being poached, why and for what exactly? A higher hourly pay? Or was she being asked to work at two places? Curiosity got the better of her, and she called the number.

A middle-aged woman answered the phone. She said she had watched Sihyeon's tutorials on YouTube and explained that she managed two convenience stores in the Dongjak district. Now, she needed someone to oversee a new store she was opening and seemed to be offering Sihyeon the manager position. Dumbfounded, Sihyeon didn't know what to say. The woman suggested that Sihyeon drop by the store to meet her in person, and then decide if they could work together. To Sihyeon's surprise, the store was very close to her home, and she agreed to visit the next day after her shift.

The owner, in her late fifties and around the same age as Mrs. Oh, couldn't be any more different from her coworker, Sihyeon had to admit. She spoke calmly and wore a kind smile. She stressed her need for a dependable manager for the new store she was opening, as she was already managing two on her own.

"How can you trust me with a whole store when you don't even know me?" Sihyeon asked cautiously. She couldn't help feeling guarded. She had never received an offer like this before, let alone a compliment.

"It was your YouTube videos," the woman explained. "I could tell by the way you speak and teach that you're more concerned about helping the learner than showing off your skills."

"Really?"

"Last month, I even trained a new part-timer by telling them to watch your videos, so I've already benefited from your help. How about you personally train our new employees at our stores? Maybe hold occasional training sessions at the new store as well. Of course, we'll cover your travel expenses."

Sihyeon bit her lip to hide her nervousness. The offer *was* for a store manager position. Hearing the salary, she gasped. Plus, the new store was just a five-minute walk from her home. She had always dreaded running into people she knew while working as a convenience store clerk, but having them see her in a manager position was a completely different story. Now, she could finally hold her head high.

She decided to accept the offer. She would stay in the same industry but move up.

As she walked home, she could feel the festive energy of Christmas

Eve in the air. The brightly decorated streets bustled with couples, but even though she was single again this Christmas, she felt far from cold.

Her new employer asked if she could start as soon as possible, as the new store would open in ten days. It meant starting the new year with a new job. That evening, flush with a mix of excitement and worry, Sihyeon waited for Mrs. Yeom to arrive. The boss usually dropped by in the evening to review the day's business with Sihyeon. Moving forward, she would need to get updates from someone else. When the boss walked in with a white paper bag, Sihyeon felt extra guilty.

"I bought some red bean buns—they're still hot. Let's have them together."

Sihyeon took one of the fish-shaped buns from the bag. She bit into the head resolutely, savoring the warmth that reminded her of Mrs. Yeom's kindness. She then shared the entire story with the boss. Mrs. Yeom stopped eating to listen to Sihyeon. After she'd heard everything, she took another bite of her bun.

"That's great."

"I'm sorry for quitting so suddenly . . ."

"No, it's good. I was worried I might be stuck with you forever. Honestly, it's a relief." She smiled.

"You're just saying that."

"You don't think I mean it?"

"No."

"Then I'll tell you the truth. I was actually considering letting you go. You know our sales have been awful. Mrs. Oh and Dokgo need more hours, so I was thinking of cutting your hours."

"What?"

"If sales drop, I have no choice but to cut back on staff. I can't lay off Mrs. Oh and Dokgo, since they rely on this job. But you—you have a home and exams coming up. As much as it would have pained me, letting you go seemed like the most logical option."

"You're kidding, right?"

"I'm serious."

"Please tell me you're joking, or I'll be really hurt."

"You need to feel that hurt so you can leave without second thoughts. Once you're somewhere else, you'll miss this place, and it'll miss you too. Missing something makes you appreciate it more, doesn't it?"

"I already appreciate this place, you know!"

Tears started to well up in Sihyeon's eyes. Her boss smiled warmly, biting down on her bun. Sihyeon chewed, holding back her tears. The sweetness of the red bean paste tickled her taste buds.

3

The Purpose of Triangle Gimbap

Oh Seonsuk had three men in her life she simply couldn't comprehend.

The first was her husband. Throughout their thirty years of marriage, she could never predict his next move. She was stunned when he suddenly quit his stable job as a section chief at a reputable company, and later again when he abruptly left home without a word, abandoning the store he had worked so hard to establish and run for several years. He was stubborn and terrible at communication. When he later fell ill and returned home, Seonsuk tried to talk to him about his selfishness, looking for answers about where he had been and why he acted this way, but he remained silent. Frustrated, she kept questioning him until he disappeared once more. Left without answers or even any way of knowing if he was alive or dead, Seonsuk gave up. Now she no longer needed to understand him.

The second man Seonsuk couldn't understand was her son. A cherished only child, he eventually became as unfathomable as her husband. At first, when he landed a corporate job straight out of university, she was thrilled that all her hard work had been rewarded. However, after just fourteen months, he abruptly quit his prestigious job and ventured into stock trading, losing all his savings. His next move was to pursue film directing. He enrolled in a school where he mingled with questionable characters, then went into debt to produce an independent film that ended up being a total flop. He became depressed and eventually had to be hospitalized.

Seonsuk couldn't understand why he would trade a stable life for high-risk pursuits like stock trading and filmmaking. Now, at her insistence, he had abandoned his fanciful ambitions and was reluctantly preparing for the foreign service exam. However, his face was still dark and troubled, and she worried he would relapse into depression. She knew it wasn't kind, but in those moments when her fear and frustration took over, it was hard for her to resist thinking: *Try lugging cement bags in the blazing sun, then see if you have any time to be depressed!*

These two men had made her life miserable. But now, another confusing man had entered her life: Dokgo, a bumbling, bearlike fool, who had started working nights at the convenience store a month ago. Initially, Seonsuk was shocked to learn that her boss had hired someone who had been homeless. But with Mrs. Yeom struggling to cover the night shifts, there were simply no other options. They had to take whatever help they could get, leaving Seonsuk little room to complain.

To her relief, Dokgo didn't cause any major problems and managed to keep the store safe through the night. He didn't smell particularly bad, and his appearance was reasonably presentable. "Don't you look nice," Mrs. Yeom would say to Dokgo, proud of the transformation he had undergone after she'd loaned him money to rent a room, buy clothes, and groom himself.

But unlike Mrs. Yeom, a lifelong teacher and the embodiment of positivity, Seonsuk held to one simple maxim: People never change. A rag, even if washed, was still a rag. Having run a bar stall in the past, she had dealt with all sorts of characters, including the twenty-year-old part-timer who stole money from the register and the sixtysomething regular who, after getting drunk and damaging property, pleaded for forgiveness, only to later bad-mouth her. As a result, Seonsuk trusted dogs more than people. Her dogs, Pretty and Blackie, showed her unwavering loyalty and devotion.

There was no way you could make her believe that the bumbling fool who had only recently shed his homeless status would ever change, regardless of how much fancy garlic ham and mugwort drinks he consumed.* Someone so antisocial and sluggish, with shifty, half-closed eyes, who struggled even to greet customers properly, could never truly fit in.

However, the impossible happened. Over the course of a single week, Dokgo didn't just change—he transformed into an upstanding member of society. He mastered all aspects of convenience store work in just three days, and within another three days, he became nimbler, bowing at customers and at Seonsuk immediately upon making eye contact. How a man who'd once struggled to even look someone in the eye managed to adapt so quickly was beyond her.

Dokgo was the third man in Seonsuk's life she couldn't understand. However, unlike with her husband and son, who both disappointed her with their inability to change, Dokgo's sudden and profound transformation utterly baffled Seonsuk. Could one small act of kindness really change someone so dramatically? If so, what in Dokgo's past made him able to adapt so quickly to his new life? Neither the boss nor Sihyeon were having any luck uncovering his past. With most of his memories lost due to alcohol-induced dementia, they had nothing to go on. Even Dokgo was a name that didn't reveal much about who he really was or where he came from.

---

* In ancient Korean mythology, there is a story about a bear that became human after eating only garlic and mugwort for a hundred days in a cave.

"Think harder, since your memory seems to be coming back a bit," Seonsuk would prompt him.

"I don't know. Thinking too hard . . . makes my head hurt . . ."

Dokgo would scrub his face with his big hands. She couldn't understand why he showed no interest in uncovering his past. Wasn't it natural, once you'd put your life back together, to wonder about your previous life, what you used to do, if you had a family, or who you really were? To Seonsuk, his lack of curiosity meant that he was still a fool—nothing but a bumbling bear of a man. And since bears weren't like dogs, he remained incomprehensible to her.

Unable to understand or trust Dokgo, Seonsuk kept her distance. However, the boss treated him as if he were a younger brother, and Sihyeon was open and comfortable with him. Whenever Seonsuk asked the girl about Dokgo during their shift change, Sihyeon maintained that he was perfectly normal. And though she didn't know what he did before becoming homeless, Sihyeon speculated that he must have been quite successful.

"Successful, my foot! Just talking to him is frustrating."

"He barely stutters now. I read somewhere that not talking can dry out your vocal cords and make you stutter. When I trained him, he seemed lost at first, but he caught on fast. It took me four days to learn everything here, but he got it in just a day or two. He even memorized all the different kinds of cigarettes in one day . . . He's definitely a quick learner."

"German shepherds learn quickly too."

"He's different. The way he acts sometimes shows real intuition, like he knows how to handle people. Look at how he deals with the PIAs, putting on that scary face. I bet he was a restaurant manager at some point."

"Pfft, more like a small-time gangster with a few thugs under him."

"I did wonder if he was from that world, but it doesn't seem like it. He doesn't give off a criminal vibe."

"Yeah, because he stayed at Seoul Station instead of a prison."

"Being homeless isn't a crime. You shouldn't be so prejudiced, Mrs. Oh."

"Not all prejudices are bad, Sihyeon. You have to be careful in this world."

Sihyeon looked like she might protest, so Seonsuk gave her a scowl that ended the conversation. The girl was too young to understand. In any case, both the boss and her young part-timer were too soft on people. Seonsuk needed to stay vigilant to make sure everything remained in order.

One morning, after preparing her son's breakfast and heading to the store for her 8:00 a.m. shift, Seonsuk found Dokgo dozing behind the cash register. He snapped awake and bowed at her. She half-heartedly acknowledged his greeting and headed to the storeroom to put on her uniform vest. When she came out, Dokgo was still standing behind the register. It wasn't until she shooed him away like a fly that he yawned and left the counter. At the POS machine, she asked, "Any issues overnight?"

"Nothing . . . too special."

"You sure?"

He scratched his head and, after a pause, answered, "Nothing's sure . . . in life."

Did she expect her to debate life's uncertainties with him? Letting out a snort at his philosophical response, she ignored him and completed her inventory check.

However, that was only the beginning of Dokgo's puzzling behavior. Although his shift ended at eight, he always stayed back, walking up and down the aisles to line up the rows of products. She wasn't sure if it was some kind of compulsion, but he would spend nearly thirty minutes at eye level with the items, sweating to get everything perfect. Didn't he want to leave as soon as his shift ended, especially when the store was empty? He seemed to get into his tidying mode only after Seonsuk got behind the cash register. But he didn't stop there. He would then head outside with cleaning gear and wipe down the table and sweep around the entrance. Afterward, he'd sit on a bench outside with a snack of expired milk and bread, watching people going to work.

Seonsuk figured Dokgo still hadn't shed his old homeless habits, and maybe he wasn't too eager to return to his little room. She shrugged it off, and before long, Dokgo would disappear, and the day would return to its normal, slow pace.

When people walk into a convenience store, they don't usually think about whether the clerk at the counter is watching them. But more people steal than one might expect, either deliberately or on impulse. They tend to let their guard down, especially when someone like Seonsuk—an older, hefty woman who doesn't move too fast—is on duty. Thanks to all her years of dealing with customers, Seonsuk had a knack for spotting suspicious characters, like the kid who just walked in. It was winter break, and the store had been seeing more middle and high school students in the mornings, but this one didn't look like he even went to school. About fifteen years old, maybe? About as tall as Seonsuk, and wearing scruffy clothes, he looked like one of those troublemakers who loitered around Wonhyoro and the electronics market.

The boy wandered through the aisles, occasionally glancing at Seonsuk. Seizing a moment when she appeared to be distracted, he quickly stuffed two triangle gimbap into his jacket. He then lingered between the aisles before finally approaching the counter. Quickly,

Seonsuk contemplated her next move. Was it worth confronting a potentially armed delinquent over a couple of gimbap? But she couldn't stand the idea of being seen as a pushover.

"Hey, lady, you got any zzamong?" he asked.

"What's zzamong? We don't carry that," Seonsuk replied. The boy turned away, uninterested in her reply.

She swiftly grabbed his arm with a practiced grip. He looked shocked, as if someone had smacked him from behind, and tried to yank his arm free.

"Empty your pockets," she said, fixing him with a glare.

The boy stood motionless.

"What do you take me for? Do it now!"

"Damn it," he muttered, reaching into his jacket with his other hand.

Seonsuk tensed, fearing he might pull out a knife. To counter her anxiety, she tightened her hold on his arm.

The boy produced a gimbap and placed it on the counter. But there was only one.

"Take it all out!" she demanded in a low, authoritative voice, just like when she scolded her dog Blackie. "Now! Before I call the police!"

Then it happened. The boy reached back into his jacket and, in one swift motion, hurled the gimbap at her face. Thud. It hit her square between the eyebrows. Dazed and momentarily blinded, she let go of his arm.

"Fuck!" he shouted.

He tried to bolt out of the store, leaving Seonsuk behind with her face tingling. But someone blocked the glass door from outside. It was Dokgo.

"Hey, Zzamong," Dokgo said, smiling at the boy as he stepped inside.

The boy, unsure of what to do, started backing away. Dokgo casually slung an arm around him in a congenial gesture and approached Seonsuk. Powerless, the boy allowed himself to be escorted to the front of the cash register. Recovering her composure, Seonsuk stepped out from behind the counter.

"This rascal . . . he forgot to pay for his stuff . . . didn't he?"

"Forgot? Yeah, right!" Seonsuk yelled. "Take him to the police station this instant!"

The boy hung his head, with Dokgo's arm firmly around his shoulders.

"Don't tell me you know this kid!" said Seonsuk, fuming.

"This is Zzamong . . . always asking for something we don't sell . . . He usually comes during my shift . . . seems he was late today. Hey, Zzamong, didn't your stomach wake you up today? Or did you sleep in?"

Dokgo spoke to the boy as if to a friend, while the boy pursed his lips and looked away. What was happening here? Had he been stealing all this time under Dokgo's watch? No, the numbers at the register had always added up. Then had the fool been secretly helping this kid all along? The admiration Seonsuk felt for Dokgo's timely intervention quickly turned to anger.

"You've been letting him get away with stealing? Tell me the truth right now!"

"He hasn't been stealing," Dokgo replied.

"I don't believe you. He tried to leave without paying. And he threw the gimbap at me!"

Dokgo turned and stood the boy up straight. He glanced at him, then at the crushed gimbap on the floor beside Seonsuk, before bending down to pick it up.

"Hey . . . is that true?"

"Yeah, so what?"

"That's . . . not okay."

Seonsuk grew more infuriated as she listened to their calm

exchange. She was the victim, yet here they were, sorting things out on their own.

Dokgo turned to her, holding out the gimbap he'd picked up from the floor along with the one from the counter. What now?

"Please ring these up."

She scoffed, but when Dokgo continued to hold out the two gimbap, she scanned them with the bar code reader. Dokgo reached into his pocket and fished out a crumpled 5,000-won bill. She accepted it as if it were a used tissue, placed it in the register, and gave him his change.

Still, Dokgo stood in front of her, the gimbap in his outstretched hand, refusing to lower it.

"You can leave now," she said.

"We're not . . . finished . . . Now throw these," Dokgo said, nodding toward the boy.

Was he suggesting that she do what the boy had done? She was dumbfounded. Dokgo's grave expression, combined with the sight of the kid standing behind him, looking as defeated as a prisoner awaiting his fate, left her speechless.

"Go on," Dokgo urged.

Things were getting out of hand. Seonsuk realized she needed to stop this nonsense.

"Do you really think I'd throw food at him?" she shrieked. "Do whatever you want—eat them or toss them, I don't care."

Dokgo chuckled. Was he laughing at her? He turned the boy around to face Seonsuk. "You've been forgiven . . . Apologize. Now."

The boy lowered his head further, showing Seonsuk the cowlick on his crown. "I'm sorry," he said in a small voice.

Seonsuk waved them off. Like a father with his son, Dokgo draped his arm around the boy's shoulders, and they exited the store. They settled at the outdoor table and began unwrapping the plastic from the gimbap. She watched as they smiled and ate together.

What had happened just now?

The real victim here was her, having been robbed and hit in the face with a rice ball. Yet, because Dokgo had resolved everything so quickly, she never got the chance to fully express her anger. Typically, she would have been seething with rage, ranting about it to anyone who would listen, but surprisingly, her anger just faded away. She was surprised to discover she didn't have much to say.

She watched Dokgo and Zzamong eat their gimbap breakfast together. Clearly, Dokgo had been looking after Zzamong all along, which explained why the rebellious boy listened to him without question. She felt something strange stir within her—a mix of relief, forgiveness, and a kind of excitement. For some strange reason, the fact that she'd been part of this bizarre drama amused her. She even considered grabbing her own triangle gimbap and joining them.

Seonsuk, despite feeling a headache coming on, couldn't help but find the change refreshingly pleasant. In short, she felt good.

As time went on, Seonsuk noticed that her frustration and bafflement with Dokgo had disappeared, replaced with an odd sense of well-being. And it wasn't just her. The store's general mood in the morning was gradually changing, like the shifting rays of the sun.

Elderly women, who usually preferred to shop at cheaper corner stores or local markets, started coming into the store as if on an outing. They would tap Dokgo on the back while he cleaned, peppering him with questions. He would then guide them around the aisles, pointing out BOGO or B2GO deals.

"If you buy these together . . . you can g-get them for cheap," he would explain. "It's a . . . great deal."

"So these end up being cheaper than at the market," one of the women noted. "I guess convenience stores aren't always overpriced. It's so nice that this man shows us all these deals."

"We can barely read the fine print. How are we supposed to know about these discounts?"

Grinning broadly, Dokgo would carry their baskets full of items to the counter and set them down in front of Seonsuk. His expression reminded her of a golden retriever expecting a treat for fetching a ball. After she rang up the purchases, to her surprise, he would leave with the women, returning with the empty baskets a short while later.

When she asked where he'd gone, he explained he'd helped carry their heavy baskets home. What kind of full service was this? Seonsuk was flabbergasted, but she couldn't deny that Dokgo's dedication to the elderly had boosted the store's morning sales. And with school on break, these grandmothers would bring their grandchildren, who were experts at getting them to open their wallets for snacks and drinks.

When Mrs. Yeom noticed the improved morning numbers, Seonsuk took all the credit, boasting about how hard she'd worked to boost sales, while keeping quiet about Dokgo's kindness to the neighborhood grandmothers and their grandkids. Of course, her conscience kicked in, so she started being a little friendlier to Dokgo.

"Are you still feeding that kid? He hasn't shown up again while I've been working."

"No, he doesn't come anymore . . . He said he was going back home."

"You believe that? I heard kids who run away from home these days all live together in some basement . . ."

"I checked . . . it was empty."

"What was empty?"

"The basement . . . where Zzamong and the others were living."

"Huh? Why'd you go there?"

"I got worried . . . But they'd all left . . . They're not there anymore."

"It's good you're thinking about those kids, but shouldn't you find a proper place for yourself first?"

"I don't need a home . . . That's why they call me homeless."

"But you're not homeless anymore, and you have a job you work hard at."

"I have . . . a long way to go."

"A long way to go where?"

"A long way . . . to everything."

"How can you be so modest? You know I'm sorry for misunderstanding you all this time, right?"

"No . . . I'm the one who's sorry . . . I'm sorry for making you misunderstand . . ."

"Anyway, you should find a studio and move. You need a proper place to sleep."

"Thank you . . . for your advice."

He nodded meekly and sauntered home, four hours after his shift had ended. Thanks to the store's increased sales and her lighter workload, Seonsuk began to trust him. It was around this time that the bearlike man started to remind her more of the dogs she trusted than the men she couldn't understand.

As the year-end approached, Mrs. Yeom announced that Sihyeon was being scouted by another convenience store in the franchise and suggested adjusting their shifts. Scouted? While Dokgo was offering free deliveries, Sihyeon was getting scouted. These part-timers were something else. Seonsuk, feeling the need to keep things in check, gladly accepted Mrs. Yeom's request for her to work more hours. Sihyeon's hours were split between Dokgo, Mrs. Yeom, and her, and she ended up working two hours longer than usual each day.

With the start of the new year and her increased workload, she tried to stay energetic, but aging another year seemed to take its toll, quickly leaving her exhausted. Her home was becoming more of a mess, and with her coming home two hours later, her son often made instant noodles for himself without cleaning up afterward. Though he claimed to be studying, the loud gaming sounds coming from his room suggested otherwise, which broke her heart.

In a nutshell, her son was only adding to the chaos at home. While she was out working, he was making no contribution to their lives. Seonsuk didn't expect him to help with the housework or be the perfect son—she just wished he would do something to improve his situation. But as the new year came and she grew more tired, her son remained an immature thirty-year-old child. He seemed resentful for having been a model student in school and not being able to enjoy his teenage years, and now he wanted to relive his life as a delinquent. The fact that a thirty-year-old, preparing for an exam, was addicted to shooting games like a teenager was truly exasperating.

Fed up, she knocked on his door, but it seemed he couldn't hear her over the noise. She tried the doorknob, but it was locked. The handle felt as cold and indifferent as her son, who only came to her when he needed something. Anger surging, she banged on the door.

"Son! Open up! I need to talk to you!!"

It wasn't until her knocking and yelling grew louder than the game that he finally opened the door, looking sullen.

"I know what you're going to say, so don't," he snapped, his tone as sharp as the gunfire from his game.

His face was greasy and dirty, and his belly hung over his shorts. He painted a pathetic picture, wearing shorts in the dead of winter because he stayed cooped up inside with the heater blasting. Gone was the smartly dressed professional. Now, he was a deadbeat. He tried to retreat, ignoring the scorn on her face, but Seonsuk grabbed his arm so tightly that her nails dug into his skin. Startled, he looked back at her, and she gripped his arm even harder, determined to confront him.

"Let me go. I need to study."

"Stop lying to me! What are you doing in there?"

"You told me to study for the foreign service exam! What's wrong with playing a few games during a break? Do you think I'm still a child? I went to a top university and worked for a major company. I know what I'm doing, so stop bothering me!"

"You ungrateful brat! Is this what you worked so hard for? To end up like this—holed up in your room, gaming, and living off ramen? Why don't you go for a walk sometimes or move into a study dorm?"

"God, I'm so sick of your constant nagging!" he yelled, wrenching his arm free.

He slammed the door shut. When she heard the click of the lock, something inside her snapped. She started banging on the door as if she intended to break it down, pounding the door in response to the way his eyes had flashed at her, as if he thought she'd lost her mind. But the only answer she received was the rising volume of gunshots from his game.

When the pounding made her hand throb, she began to bang her forehead against the door. Thud. Thud, thud. Thud, thud. When her forehead grew numb, she finally gave up and turned away. Tears streamed down her face, and her heart ached, but there was no husband to share this burden. She couldn't even turn to her friends. How could she, when she had always boasted about her son? The distant echoes of her classmates' gossip, the ones who had envied her when her son was hired at a major company, seemed to ring in her ears.

Even after crying herself to sleep, she woke up at seven as usual. Incredibly, the sounds of gaming were still coming from her son's room. She threw on her coat and left the house without making breakfast, desperate to escape. But the only place she could go to was work.

When she stepped inside the store, Dokgo wasn't at the counter. She turned around and saw that he was lining up a new display of noodle bowls. Even though she had told him it wasn't necessary, he obsessively aligned each product. His behavior was in stark contrast to her hopeless son.

"Hello," Dokgo greeted her.

Seonsuk couldn't respond properly as tears suddenly filled her eyes. She rushed to the storeroom and changed into her uniform, but the tears wouldn't stop. Her son's situation seemed worse than that of a middle-aged man who had only recently escaped homelessness. No, Dokgo was now a respectable member of society, wasn't he? In contrast, her son was addicted to games, a lost soul with a bleak future. He was just like his father. And if something were to happen to Seonsuk, she feared he might end up homeless or a vagrant. These thoughts overwhelmed her until she sank to the floor, sobbing.

When she finally came to her senses, she saw Dokgo standing at the storeroom door, watching her. He walked over and offered his hand. She took it and stood up. He then handed her some tissues, which she used to wipe her tears and nose. Feeling as if a dam inside her had broken, she took deep breaths to calm herself.

Dokgo led her out of the storeroom, where the bright morning light was streaming in through the large window. He went to the cooler and brought back a bottle of corn silk tea.

"Corn silk tea's the best when . . . when you're upset," he said, pouring her a cup.

Puzzled, Seonsuk gazed at the kindness placed before her. She needed something to quell her rising emotions. She gulped it down like a cold beer on a hot summer day.

Once her thirst was quenched, she couldn't hold back any longer. Dokgo listened intently as if he had been waiting for her to open up. Standing at the counter, Seonsuk poured out her woes about her pathetic son, wiping away tears, while Dokgo listened and nodded.

"I don't get it. Why would he throw away a perfectly good job and waste his life on ridiculous things? Aren't stocks and movie production the same as gambling? Where did my son go wrong?"

"He's still . . . young."

"He's thirty! And a total deadbeat!"

"Have you tried . . . talking to him?"

"He won't listen. He just brushes me off. I've tried so many times, but he shuts me out and now he's avoiding me. To him, I'm nothing but a maid and landlord!"

"First, listen . . . to your son. You say he doesn't listen, b-but . . . sounds like you don't listen to him either."

"What do you mean?"

"You're listening to me right now . . . Try listening to him too. Ask him why . . . why he quit his job . . . why he got into stocks . . . why he made a movie . . . stuff like that."

"What's the point? He's already ruined everything. I told you he won't even talk to me!"

"But there must have been a time . . . when he tried to tell you."

"It's been three years. When he said he was quitting his job, I lost it. I mean, why leave a perfectly good job, right?"

"So do you know why . . . he quit?"

"I told you I don't."

"Ask him again . . . Find out why. Why . . . it was hard for him. Only your son knows. You should know, too . . . since it's about him."

"I blew up because I was scared. I told him to tough it out. But he went ahead and quit anyway. Just like his dad when he walked out on us."

Seonsuk poured out her story, her eyes welling up again. She tried to hold back her tears, worried about how she might look to Dokgo. He paused, his cheeks twitching, then offered her a gentle smile.

"You were scared . . . he'd turn out like his dad."

Seonsuk's tears stopped. She found herself nodding. "You're right. I thought my son would be different . . . Maybe it's my fault . . . I did everything I could, but he just doesn't see it . . . He's always holed up in his room, playing games—" she said, her voice cracking with emotion.

Dokgo handed her some more tissues. She quickly wiped her tears as a customer entered. Dokgo retreated to the storeroom while Seonsuk composed herself and stepped behind the counter to help the customer.

Once the customer left and Dokgo returned, Seonsuk, now calmer, smiled sheepishly at him.

"I went on quite a bit, didn't I? I've been struggling, and I didn't have anyone to talk to. I feel better now after telling you everything. Thank you."

"That's it."

"Huh?"

"When someone listens . . . it makes you feel better."

Seonsuk's eyes widened as she took in his words.

"Try listening to your son. It'll . . . make things better. Even if it's just a bit."

It was then that Seonsuk realized she had never truly listened to her son. She'd always wanted him to live as she wanted, without ever hearing his struggles or understanding why he strayed from the path she'd planned. She'd been too focused on scolding him for his mistakes to see why he made those choices.

"Here . . ." Dokgo placed a set of three triangle gimbap on the counter, a B2GO deal.

Seonsuk stared, puzzled.

"For your son," he said with a smile.

"For my son? Why?"

"Zzamong says . . . triangle gimbap's the best when you're gaming . . . Give it to him while he plays."

Seonsuk stared at the triangle gimbap. Her son had always liked them. When she first started working at the store, he'd asked her to bring back the ones they couldn't sell. But at some point, Seonsuk had stopped. She hadn't liked seeing him eat them alone in his room, absorbed in his games. As she looked on, lost in thought, Dokgo's murmur reached her ears.

"But these . . . aren't enough. Write him a letter . . . Add it to the gimbap."

Seonsuk looked up. Dokgo was gazing straight at her, and at that moment, he really did seem like a golden retriever.

"Write him . . . and tell him you didn't listen before . . . but you will now. Ask him to tell you . . . and give these with the letter."

Seonsuk bit her lip, gazing at the gimbap before her. Dokgo pulled out three crumpled 1,000-won bills from his pocket.

"They're on me . . . Please scan them."

As if following a command, Seonsuk moved the bar code reader over the gimbap. When she heard the beep and the machine's voice announce, "Transaction completed," she felt a sense of peace settle over the chaos in her mind. Seonsuk, who once trusted dogs more than people, nodded at Dokgo, who smiled and turned to leave the store. As the door chimed, Seonsuk began to think about what she would write to her son.

4

BOGO

In Kyeongman's mind, the convenience store was like a bird feeder. *Off to the feeder again*, he would think, seeing himself as the bird. When he was young, there was a hit song called "Day of a Sparrow." Song Chang-sik, in his famous warbling voice, compared ordinary people to sparrows, offering comfort for life's struggles. "Dawn is breaking. Today once again, I go out to get my grain. Dawn is breaking." Even when he was a young boy in elementary school, the words had resonated with Kyeongman, and he'd often found himself humming along. Not much had changed since then. He still felt like that boy who dreaded school, viewing life as an endless series of days to endure.

While to some, solitary drinking seemed romantic or trendy, for Kyeongman, it was simply a bottle of soju consumed alone at the convenience store's patio table while braving the cold wind. *Romantic, my foot*. He considered himself lucky not to receive disdainful looks from those passing by.

He couldn't pinpoint when the table at Always Convenience became his private watering hole. When the colder weather set in, he would stop for a bowl of instant noodles before heading home.

Like most late-night snacks, that routine soon expanded—first to include a triangle gimbap, then some stir-fried kimchi, and finally a bottle of Jinro soju, creating a proper feast. Kyeongman became a regular, a bird that couldn't escape the feeder, warming his insides with 5,000 won's worth of drinks and side dishes every night. The cold soju and hot soup always heated him up from the inside. The variety of noodle bowls and triangle gimbap offered endless combinations that never grew dull. Tonight, it was So-So-So, a favorite for the past few months: somyeon noodles, soboro triangle gimbap, and soju—not only an unbeatable way to end his day, but also a budget-friendly choice for his solo drinking sessions.

Tonight, however, an intimidating new man stood behind the counter, practically the opposite of the previous worker, who'd been like the roly-poly Anpanman. Kyeongman awkwardly placed his soju bottle, noodle bowl, and gimbap on the counter, and the man rang them up slowly, as if he had all the time in the world.

"That'll be . . . fifty-two hundred won," he said in a gruff voice.

Kyeongman quickly paid and grabbed some wooden chopsticks before heading out to the table. He set the food down and took out the paper cup he always carried for soju. Now, all that remained was to prepare the somyeon. As he peeled off the noodle lid, he made the mistake of glancing inside the store and made eye contact with the bearlike man. He quickly looked away and tore open the soup mix. Going back inside for hot water, he thought about the previous worker, who had been there until last week. Likely a retiree who was working part time, he had a round face and clean-shaven head, which had made Kyeongman nickname him Anpanman. Anpanman had been very kind, handing him wooden chopsticks with the instant noodles and wishing him "Bon appétit" every time. Sometimes, he'd even offered Kyeongman sandwiches slightly past their expiry date for free, assuring him they were perfectly fine to eat.

Kyeongman had cherished those moments of peaceful camaraderie during the quiet hours, a shared understanding between individuals battling life on the front lines.

So who was this new man who had taken Anpanman's place? Kyeongman pondered this as he waited for his noodles to cook. The man's gruff manner, his apparent inexperience in customer service, and his aloof, almost haughty gaze, as if he judged Kyeongman for his solitary drinking—this was someone accustomed to authority. That was it. He was the convenience store boss, no different from the CEO of Kyeongman's company, who made his life a living hell. Perhaps the man at the counter had fired Anpanman due to declining business. Lacking a better alternative, he'd employed a neighborhood grandma for a few days, but it obviously hadn't worked out, so he'd had no choice but to step in himself. Kyeongman guessed that Anpanman was let go just shy of his one-year mark, so that the boss wouldn't have to fork over severance pay. His own company always laid off temps around the eleventh month, regardless of their performance.

Kyeongman started to develop a nice buzz. He blew on the hot noodles and washed a mouthful down with a shot of soju, thinking about bosses. The economy had been in the dumps for ages, and work was perpetually challenging. His CEO, citing financial difficulties, had scrapped the bonuses for Chuseok, only to upgrade to a new luxury car. Meanwhile, Kyeongman's salary had been frozen for four years, a topic of ridicule among his juniors. Treated as expendable, yet financially unable to resign, he viewed his CEO as a dictator.

And it wasn't like he could escape this hell when he went home. With his twins entering middle school next year, the family expenses were going up, and his wife, burdened with part-time work and household responsibilities, had little time for him. The warmth, security, and support one expected to feel at home had vanished, and even soju had been cut from his regular nightcap and late-night snacks for quite some time. His wife refused to let him drink at home, convinced it was bad for the children to be around alcohol. Even his one hobby, watching baseball highlights, was off-limits now that the kids had claimed control of the TV remote. Overworked and underpaid, he couldn't fully devote himself to his family, nor could he command their respect with his paltry salary. Kyeongman felt like a failure, certain he would grow old as an insignificant husband and a dull father. No, if he got fired and couldn't find another job, even this fragile existence would crumble.

Where did it all go wrong? He had done his best for the past forty-four years. After graduating from an unremarkable college, he had ventured into a challenging field, pharmaceutical sales. He then went on to insurance, automotive, paper, and medical equipment sales, accumulating experience without ever straying from his path. Born without privilege, he had leaned on sincerity and kindness as his core strengths. When he married his wife, a former client four years his junior, and they welcomed twins into the world, he believed that his modest life was beautiful and precious, that affluence didn't matter.

However, time revealed a harsher reality. Those who'd had a head start in life continued to prosper, amassing skills and wealth, while Kyeongman felt like a soldier in the trenches who had run out of ammunition and was now forced to charge into an open battlefield. No matter how much he earned, expenses always soared, while his energy drained away. His physical stamina, the bedrock of his sincerity and kindness, ebbed with age, turning these virtues into incompetence and subservience. Even his mental strength began to erode, until his boss and coworkers lost respect for him.

Lost in these bitter thoughts, he drank and drank until he realized he had only half a shot left. The egg block in his noodles hadn't fully dissolved, and he was almost out of soju—a real dilemma. But another bottle would make tomorrow unbearable. Gone were the days of his youth when he could down three or four bottles and head to work without a hangover. These days, more than a bottle meant he might vomit on the subway during the morning rush.

Resilience—that's what he had lost. In his younger years, he could bounce back from mistakes and shake off hangovers with a hot shower. Now, that resilience was fading like everything else. Kyeongman swallowed the final bite of gimbap, slurped down the remaining noodles, and knocked back the last of his soju. After savoring his only moment of freedom that day, he tidied up and left.

The next night, the bearlike man rang up Kyeongman's items with the same indifference. This time, however, he promptly included the chopsticks. He was a fast learner. Maybe that's why he'd been able to become a convenience store owner, despite being no older than Anpanman. He likely led a comfortable life, having built his wealth early while others his age faced layoffs. Kyeongman guessed he now managed several stores, stepping in for part-timers as needed.

Feeling a mix of envy and helplessness, Kyeongman completed the one small ritual that still brought him some pleasure. The owner was still watching him. How did he view Kyeongman? Probably as a loser, a struggling family man. But it didn't matter. He was still a customer, a model one in fact, who spent 5,000 won every day and cleaned up after himself. The owner's gaze felt oppressive, but Kyeongman was determined not to relinquish his place in this corner of the world.

More than a month passed this way. The year was drawing to a close. *Damn it.* In 2019, not only was there no promotion, but Kyeongman would be lucky to avoid a salary cut. He was already panicking about his daughters starting middle school in March, and his wife had begun cautiously mentioning that the girls would need to attend more cram schools. On these cold nights, drinking soju at the outdoor table seemed to be the only way Kyeongman could relieve his stress.

He wasn't sure exactly when the owner came and sat down at the table. Had he dozed off, huddled over from the cold, fatigue, and alcohol? When he opened his eyes, the boss was sitting in front of him, a polar bear in his white jacket, his breath visible in the chilly air.

"Hey, mister. If you fall asleep here . . . you'll freeze . . . to death."

The boss was treating Kyeongman as if he were homeless. He felt a surge of anger, but intimidated by the owner's size and presence, he quietly poured the rest of the soju into his paper cup.

"Drinking . . . doesn't keep . . . the cold away," said the owner in his usual halting way.

Kyeongman wasn't sure if the owner was simply distracted or being casually bourgeois, but either way, his manner of speaking got on his nerves. Kyeongman emptied his cup.

"Well, I feel warmer. I'll be off after I finish this, so no need to rush me," he said in a small act of defiance as he reached for the soju bottle. But the bottle was empty! Embarrassment and annoyance swept over him. He couldn't drink more even if he wanted to, and he especially didn't want to appear weak before this man. But right then, the owner said, "Just a moment," and disappeared into the store. What now?

He returned with two large coffee cups. Kyeongman watched in surprise as the man placed one cup in front of him. It was filled with a light amber liquid and two ice cubes, oddly resembling whiskey. Kyeongman was convinced it was whiskey. But why? Could it be

poisoned? He eyed the owner warily. The man gestured for Kyeongman to drink, then took a sip from his own cup leisurely, an action
that seemed all too familiar to him. It reminded Kyeongman of his
days in pharmaceutical sales, watching doctors and professors casually drinking whiskey bombs as though they were barley tea.

When Kyeongman remained motionless, the man picked up his
cup and finished it, leaving only the ice cubes.

"Kyah . . ." He licked his lips in satisfaction, prompting Kyeongman to finally drink his own cup, which he finished in one go. The
cold liquid seemed to freeze his esophagus and chest. Unlike whiskey, there was no burning sensation, only a chilling cold.

"Refreshing, isn't it?"

"What is this?"

"It's corn . . . silk tea. It's good . . . when you're upset."

Corn silk tea with ice . . . Kyeongman was shocked.

"The color . . . makes it feel like you're drinking . . . and it's also
good for settling your stomach."

Kyeongman couldn't tell if the man was simply odd or mocking
him. However, he couldn't exactly be angry about being offered a nonalcoholic beverage. He forced himself to nod and began tidying up.

"I used to drink . . . every day too," the man murmured.

Kyeongman paused, suddenly more aware of the man before
him, and sat back down.

"When I drank every day . . . everything started to fall apart. My
body, my head . . ." He trailed off.

Kyeongman felt uneasy. He was the one drinking, yet the other
man was the one acting drunk. As he prepared to leave, he quickly
asked, "So what are you saying? That I should stop coming here?"

The man reached into his jacket. Was he pulling out a knife?
Kyeongman tensed, but instead, the man brought out a bottle of
corn silk tea and held it up.

"Drink corn silk tea instead . . . Here, have some more," he said, unscrewing the cap.

He poured the tea into their cups, which now contained nothing but ice, as if Kyeongman were an old drinking buddy. To Kyeongman's disbelief, the man then raised his cup for a toast. What the hell was this? Out of habit, Kyeongman bumped his cup slightly lower than the man's and downed it in one gulp. The drink was cold.

"I think the alcohol I used to drink . . . was this color," the man said, setting down his cup.

You're probably right. And you probably drank plenty of whiskey, made a boatload of money, and now, as a boss, you're looking after your health and enjoying your second act.

"But now . . . this is all I drink. You can live without alcohol."

"Are you telling me I should quit drinking?"

The man nodded, his expression blank. A surge of irritation shot through Kyeongman.

"Why don't you just tell me to stop coming here? Why are you telling me to quit drinking?"

"I want to help . . . I'll bring you this tea with ice. Have it with your noodles and gimbap. Then you won't think about drinking anymore."

"Have I ever caused any trouble here? Or left a mess? I always clean up after myself. What kind of help are you talking about? If you don't want me to come, just say so."

Kyeongman stood up and walked away without looking back. *Let that nutjob clean up the table himself.* It felt like a business relationship that had ended. There was no longer any need to make a good impression or care. He couldn't tell if the cold tea was clearing his head or if the chilly night air was waking him up. As confusion swirled, Kyeongman tried to stifle the sadness of losing his little haven.

By the end of the year, with constant work dinners, Kyeongman came home drunk every other day. He didn't miss drinking alone at the convenience store. Even when he passed by on his way home from the subway station, he gave it only a cursory glance through bleary eyes. He walked past the deserted outdoor table, satisfied that the boss had lost him as a customer.

The year 2020 arrived. People ditched the old year, as if tossing dirty clothes into the wash and slipping into fresh ones. His wife and the twins, on the brink of middle school, welcomed the new year with energy. The twins had grown to his shoulders, and he realized he'd soon be the shortest in the family. (Before marriage, both he and his wife had been five foot five, but while she stayed the same, his latest health check revealed he'd apparently shrunk to five foot four.)

His shrinking height wasn't the only issue. Every new year chipped away at his self-esteem. He faced humiliations at work and a growing sense of alienation at home. Sure, quitting his job might restore some of his wounded pride, but he didn't know how to fix feeling invisible at home. What if he quit his job and left home? He'd probably end up homeless.

This year, Kyeongman's goal was to leave his thankless job and find something new. His wife would worry, but he longed to work in a place where he'd be treated decently, even if it meant earning less. Then again, a smaller paycheck might mean he'd be treated worse at home. To him, the new year just felt like an extension of the same old winter. Wasn't January 2020 just as cold as December 2019? He couldn't understand people's feverish excitement for the new year and shook his head at the relentless New Year's marketing everywhere.

He was itching for a drink. But of his three drinking buddies, two had made New Year's resolutions to quit alcohol, and the third had returned to his hometown to take up farming. Even the work party to kick off the new year was in line with the times—everyone just wanted to have lunch, having already partied hard at the year-end bash. Kyeongman felt like the whole world was leaving him behind. His sense of loneliness and isolation only fueled his craving for alcohol.

An outcast always drinks alone. But he didn't have the budget or the heart to splurge on solo drinking at a bar. Frustratingly, the only place in his area that kept its outdoor table during winter was Always Convenience, with that oddball owner in the polar-bear jacket who sipped corn silk tea like it was whiskey. The guy was such a weirdo that he didn't even hire a night-shift worker and kept watch over the store himself. Damn it, shouldn't an owner be creating jobs? Grumbling, he was about to walk past the store when he stopped.

To his surprise, there was a bowl of instant somyeon sitting on the outdoor table.

Oh, how he missed So-So-So! It seemed like the only thing that could comfort him in this dreary, monotonous new year. So-So-So had the power to throw open the doors to a fresh start. He couldn't resist. Even if the noodle bowl was bait set by the Polar Bear to lure him in, Kyeongman didn't care. Telling himself that if the Polar Bear decided to crash his So-So-So drinking session, he'd figure out a way to fend him off, he went inside, grabbed his gimbap and soju, and filled the noodle bowl with hot water.

"Ah . . . long time no see," the owner said, as he leisurely rang up the items.

Kyeongman nodded silently and quickly stepped outside. Unfazed by the cold, he closed the lid on the noodles to let them cook, tore open the triangle gimbap, and unscrewed the cap of the soju bottle. Damn it, he didn't have a cup. He had recently removed the little paper cups he used for soju from his bag. It was annoying to buy new ones, and he certainly wasn't going to ask the Polar Bear for help. Fine, who needed a cup anyway? He could just drink straight from the bottle, right?

Just then, the owner came outside. Kyeongman, trying to act nonchalant, was startled by what appeared to be a fan in the man's hand. On closer inspection, it turned out to be a dish heater. The owner plugged it into an outlet Kyeongman hadn't noticed before and placed it beside him, turning it on.

Confused, Kyeongman watched as the owner gestured for him to enjoy the warmth before heading back inside. Despite his bewilderment, the heater's warmth began to thaw Kyeongman's frozen expression. Whether his face was stiff from the winter wind or from embarrassment, it quickly relaxed.

"I've got only this cup here . . ."

The Polar Bear came back out, offering a paper coffee cup. Kyeongman silently accepted it. He felt he needed to say something.

"Thank you."

"For what?"

"For the cup . . . and the heater."

"You didn't come for a while . . . so I thought I wouldn't get to use it."

"You mean the heater?"

"I got it because you used to sit out here . . . I figured you weren't coming because of the cold . . . so I got one . . . Anyway, I'm glad you came."

Despite his usual gruff manner, the Polar Bear's words were even warmer than the heater. He disappeared inside as Kyeongman continued to drink, unaware his noodles were getting mushy.

Everything was warm—the soju, the cup, and the heater the owner had purchased just for him. Kyeongman may have been an outcast elsewhere, but not here. Here, it turned out, he was welcome. He felt like a VIP making a comeback.

He quickly finished the So-So-So. He wanted to linger in the warmth, but forced himself to get up, just as the owner appeared again, as if expecting something. In one hand, he held a paper cup, presumably with ice, and in the other, a bottle of corn silk tea. *Oh my God.*

Still, the owner was at least ten years older, so Kyeongman felt obliged to show some respect. He figured he just needed to drink one round, like he would with a client. Kyeongman held the cup with both hands, accepting the tea.

"It's tough, isn't it?"

Kyeongman nodded. But the owner, rubbing his chin with his large hand, asked, "What kind of work . . . keeps you out this late?"

Wait, he does me a favor and now he's prying into my life?

"I work in sales."

"Sales . . . What do you sell?"

It's not like you can buy what I'm selling.

"Medical equipment."

"Medical equipment? So . . . you supply hospitals?"

Why? Do you own a hospital or something?

"Yes, we do."

"Then it must be tough . . . You're the breadwinner, right? When I look at you . . . I can sense the weight of responsibility."

Now you want to get into my personal life too? Isn't this crossing a line, mister?

"Sir, you seem like the breadwinner yourself," Kyeongman said. "Life's not easy."

"If you get off work this late . . . you must hardly see your kids. Let me guess . . . you have a daughter at home?"

What is he—a fortune teller? To be fair, he had a fifty-fifty chance of getting that right.

"Two daughters."

"That's great. Daughters are ... the best."

The owner rubbed his face with his thick hands. For some reason, the gesture seemed lonely, and Kyeongman's irritation softened. Almost instinctively, he pulled out his wallet. Inside, there was a photo of his twin daughters, grinning with shiny teeth, taken when they had just entered elementary school six years ago. He saw this picture more often than he saw them in person these days.

"They're so lovely ... I can't tell who's who," the man said.

"They're twins."

"Ah, I see ... That's why you work so hard ... for these lovely girls."

"Don't all parents do that?"

"Being a parent ... it's tough, isn't it?"

"Yes."

Even though Kyeongman knew these were leading questions, he felt compelled to respond. Like a dam breaking, words started pouring out of him uncontrollably. He talked about his daughters, soon-to-be middle schoolers who barely spoke to him, his wife's constant complaints, the diminishing respect at work, and finally the humiliations he faced in client meetings ... As if confessing, Kyeongman told the man everything, impassioned, spittle flying.

The man poured him another cup of corn silk tea. Thirsty, Kyeongman gulped it down. He felt refreshed inside, but soon a wave of embarrassment hit.

"It's not easy ... to quit your job," the owner said. "And you don't get enough time with your family ... and no way to ease the pain ... So, that's why ... you drink here after work."

"Yes."

"Then . . . drink corn silk tea instead."

"Pardon me?"

"Quit drinking and have corn silk tea instead . . . Didn't your wife ban alcohol at home? If you drink corn silk tea . . . you won't feel guilty and you can enjoy a late-night snack at home . . . w-with your family."

"What are you talking about?"

"I quit drinking too . . . just two months ago . . . This . . . made it possible."

The man acted as if he had invented the beverage himself and tried to pour Kyeongman some more. However, Kyeongman quickly stood up, grabbing his bag.

"Thank you," he said, bowing before leaving, but the man's voice followed him.

"When you don't drink, you're fresh . . . the next day . . . and you become more productive."

Obviously. My productivity goes up, then my salary, then my position, and I hit the jackpot. Who doesn't know that? What a load of bullcrap. Why don't you go drown in your beloved corn silk tea?

After that ridiculous conversation, Kyeongman started taking the long way home to avoid the Polar Bear at the convenience store. It meant climbing ten more steps and passing through a dark alley where the snow still hadn't melted, but it was worth it as long as he didn't have to see that preachy old man's face. He vowed never to drink at that convenience store again.

But without Always Convenience, he now had nowhere to go. He tried a few cheap bars, but their seedy atmosphere only worsened his mood. And none of the other convenience stores in the neighborhood put out their outdoor tables until spring.

Screw it. Kyeongman decided to go straight home without

drinking. When he arrived before eleven, without the smell of alcohol on him, his wife and daughters, initially surprised, quickly became supportive of what they assumed was a New Year's resolution to quit drinking. A New Year's resolution to quit drinking? They had misunderstood, but even so, their support felt good. He decided he might as well quit drinking. That made him eager to get home earlier, and soon he forgot about drinking alone.

Instead of watching baseball, he started watching TV programs after work with his family, discovering many interesting shows. Particularly on Wednesdays, he made sure he was home early to watch *Let's Eat Dinner Together*. His older daughter lamented that the show never visited Cheongpa-dong and wished cohost Kang Ho-dong would come to their house dressed as Santa Claus. The younger one, born five minutes after her sister, preferred the other cohost, Lee Kyung-kyu. She often asked for Don Chicken after seeing the ad featuring him as Don Quixote. On such days, even his wife didn't mind ordering fried chicken, and the daughters were happy to have Dad home so they could enjoy the food together.

Were they happy about the fried chicken or about him? It didn't matter. Biting into the chicken together—that was what family was all about.

That year, during the Lunar New Year holiday, Kyeongman didn't touch a drop of alcohol even when they visited his parents. His father and uncles, who usually got drunk and played Go-Stop during the holidays, treated him as if he were being pretentious, but his wife and mother smiled warmly.

A few days later, on his way home from work late at night, Kyeongman found himself taking the shortcut that passed by the convenience store. Now, walking past the store no longer triggered his craving for a drink, and his steps felt almost natural. Still, he couldn't help glancing toward the store, curious if the Polar Bear was still working the night shift, unable to find a part-timer.

There was no one at the counter. Only a bottle of corn silk tea sat on the outdoor table. *What an interesting man the Polar Bear is,* Kyeongman thought. He stared at the bottle for a moment, then picked it up and went inside.

Ding-dong.

The store was empty, eerily quiet. Kyeongman felt an irresistible urge to drink the corn silk tea. But there was no one at the counter. It felt more like an inconvenience store than a convenience store.

Just then, the Polar Bear emerged from the storeroom, stretching as if waking from hibernation. He spotted Kyeongman, grinned, and made his way to the counter. Feeling a bit embarrassed, Kyeongman figured he should say something and asked, "How have you been?"

"Fine . . . How about you?"

"Good, thanks to you."

An awkward silence followed. Kyeongman finally put down the bottle of corn silk tea.

"How much is it?"

"It's on the house."

"Why?"

"I left it out for you."

"But why?"

"Well . . . I told you before . . . corn silk tea is as addictive as a- alcohol," the man said with a grin. "If you drink two or three a day . . . it's good for our sales. So it's basically . . . bait."

It sounded ridiculous, but Kyeongman decided to play along.

"Well, thank you," Kyeongman said with a polite nod.

"And why don't you . . . buy these instead?" the man added, pointing.

Kyeongman turned to see a display of Loacker chocolates right in front of the counter.

"Yes, those," the man continued. "We're having a . . . buy-one-get-one deal on them right now."

Sure enough, there was a "1+1" sticker next to the chocolates. Kyeongman placed two on the counter as instructed.

"The loveliest girls in Cheongpa-dong . . . two identical lovely girls . . . they really like these," the man said in his casual tone while ringing up the purchase, but Kyeongman's heart raced. He handed over his card, his mouth suddenly dry.

"They used to buy these all the time . . . but recently, they've just been getting the BOGO chocolate milk . . . So I asked them . . . Don't you girls like these anymore?"

"And what did they say?" Kyeongman asked, trying to sound calm.

"One of them . . . don't know if it was the older or younger one . . . said it wasn't a BOGO deal anymore . . ."

Kyeongman didn't say anything. The man handed him back his card. Kyeongman barely managed to take it, speechless.

"So . . . I tested them," the man said slowly. "I said, 'Kids, these don't cost that much. Ask your mom to get them for you.' And do you know what they said?"

"What did they say?" Kyeongman asked, feeling like he might suffocate from how slowly the man spoke.

"They said their mother told them . . . 'Since Dad works hard to make money . . . you should save . . . and only buy things on buy-one-get-one deals.' That's what they said . . . Gosh, so smart with money . . . such good heads on their shoulders . . . I thought . . . whoever raised them did a great job."

Kyeongman was moved by how much his family cared for him.

"Starting yesterday . . . these chocolates are back on a BOGO deal . . . so you can get them today . . . And tomorrow . . . tell your daughters to come and buy them."

Seeing the tears rolling down Kyeongman's face, the man let out a chuckle and tapped the counter a few times. Kyeongman wiped his tears with his coat sleeve, bowed to the man, and opened his wallet to put his card away. Inside his wallet, his daughters' smiling faces looked back at him—his very own buy-one-get-one deal.

5

The Inconvenience Store

Life was a series of problems to be solved. Inkyeong trudged along a sidewalk that was too worn and bumpy for wheeling luggage. Her trunk rattled behind her as she scanned her surroundings. Today's main objective was to find her winter accommodation. Fortunately, securing a place to stay wasn't the problem, she had already done that. Now she had to figure out where it was. For someone with a poor sense of direction, navigating the intricate alleys of Seoul's older neighborhoods was no easy feat. She had used her map app to get from Namyeong Station to Cheongpa Church, but after turning onto a back street behind the church, her iPhone shut down. Winter was coming! And with it, her ancient iPhone went into unexpected hibernation, further complicating her quest. Now, she couldn't even call for directions. "Ah sh—" Biting back a curse, Inkyeong realized she needed to ask for help.

Spotting a convenience store at a small three-way intersection between side streets, Inkyeong mustered her remaining energy and dragged her trunk there. Wouldn't a convenience store offer some convenience? She left her trunk near the doors and grabbed a chocolate bar from a display. Behind the counter, a tall woman in her twenties stood watching her.

Inkyeong paid for the chocolate, tore open the wrapper, and bit into it. The sugar hit helped steady her trembling limbs, exhausted from dragging the luggage. Under the clerk's gaze, she polished off the entire bar. Then, as casually as she could, she asked, "Could I make a quick phone call?"

The clerk consented, and Inkyeong bowed gratefully. She awkwardly laid her trunk down on the floor and opened it. Thankfully, she'd written the number in her notebook.

Dialing from the store's landline, she introduced herself to the young woman who answered and explained that she'd had to call from the convenience store because her phone battery was dead.

"Convenience store? Are you at Always by any chance?"

When Inkyeong said yes, the girl on the phone laughed, saying she was on the third floor of the low-rise building right across from the store. Inkyeong hung up and peered outside. A third-floor window slid open, and a girl, face beaming with a familiar smile, waved at her.

Inkyeong had spent the autumn at the Park Kyongni Toji Cultural Center in Wonju, a facility established by the late author of the renowned novel *Toji*, Park Kyongni. The center was designed to support future generations of writers and artists by offering them a space to work, as well as three meals a day, free of charge. It was Inkyeong's first visit as a writer, and there, she planned to bring her writing career to a close.

She had moved out of her rental in Daehangno, Seoul's theater district, sent all her belongings to her parents' house, and arrived at the center with just one trunk. Nestled in the woods of a quiet village on the outskirts of Wonju, the center was a hidden retreat for writers—an ideal place for solitude, free from distractions. There, she took daily walks along trails perfect for clearing and organizing her thoughts and enjoyed meals made from healthy ingredients. The center's quiet rhythm was a refreshing change, with each writer moving in their own orbit, exchanging cautious glances with one another. While some enjoyed table tennis after lunch or gathered for makgeolli by the stream after dinner, Inkyeong, usually outgoing, chose solitude.

She had come with one purpose in mind: to quit writing for good if she couldn't manage to write there. However, spending time alone didn't make writing any easier, but she wasn't overly anxious either. Writing had always been a challenge, and even if she finished something, there was no guarantee it would make it to the stage, so she simply endured. She asked herself if she could continue living as a playwright, and these thoughts deepened with the autumn leaves.

After about three weeks at the center, Huisu approached her. A seasoned novelist and literature professor from a university in Gwangju, Huisu was on sabbatical, visiting literary centers at home and abroad, with the Toji Cultural Center as her last stop. She had taken particular notice of Inkyeong, who, like a hermit, had holed up in the writing room, wrestling with the potential end of her career.

"Coming to a writer's retreat to give up on writing? Sounds like something out of a book. Or maybe some absurdist play?"

"It's just . . . I'm out of options. I think I've hit my limit. I've kept my head down and worked hard to push through, but to be honest, I'm worn out."

"Then take a break. Park Kyongni once said that even if the writers here look like they're not working and just goofing off, it's all part of the process, so let them be. Let go of what's weighing you down and just think about your work while you rest. Remember, mindless typing isn't the same as writing."

"Thank you, Professor. I've never had any formal training in writing, so I really appreciate your advice."

"Oh, please, just call me Huisu. And next time you go for a walk, don't go alone. Let's go together, okay?"

That's how Huisu had comforted Inkyeong on their first walk. After that, they often walked together, strolling along the lake pathway on the Yonsei University campus near the center and exploring nearby forest trails. By the end of their residency, they even climbed Mount Chiak together, and Inkyeong felt she had gained a true friend she was reluctant to part with.

A week before leaving the center, Huisu asked where Inkyeong was headed next. Inkyeong admitted that, despite writing little during her stay, she felt recharged and planned to return to Seoul to find a new place to write. She'd put her retirement as a writer on temporary hold, and if that was her only achievement during the residency, so be it. Since her dreams had started in Seoul, she was determined to realize them there. Huisu nodded in understanding.

"So where are you planning to stay while you write?" Huisu asked.

Inkyeong was thinking about checking into a goshiwon. Since she lacked both money and resolve, a small dorm seemed like her only option. She said that if she couldn't produce something over the winter, she would quit for good and return to her hometown in Busan, where she could join the family business at Bupyeong Kkangtong Market or work at friends' shops. Her parents would probably set her up on dates with potential suitors, and if she didn't resist, marriage and children would most likely follow.

"If I go home, I can do everything . . . except write," Inkyeong said shyly, to which Huisu responded with an awkward smile.

The next day, Huisu asked Inkyeong if she would consider staying somewhere other than a goshiwon. She offered her daughter's empty apartment near Sookmyung Women's University, as her daughter was coming home to Gwangju for the winter break. Noting the surprise on Inkyeong's face, Huisu explained that the apartment would only be available for three months, since her daughter would return to school in March. She hoped Inkyeong could use the space to write comfortably, offering it for free, as if Inkyeong were doing her a favor. Touched by the professor's generosity, Inkyeong, usually stoic, nearly broke down in tears. She beamed at the professor in response.

It felt like she'd been given another writing retreat—one that might again become her last. And this place that could mark the end of her life in Seoul, as a writer, and as a theater person, was an apartment on the third floor of a low-rise in Cheongpa-dong, Yongsan.

"My mom said to show you around the neighborhood," Huisu's daughter said when she met Inkyeong at the door. "But my boyfriend's coming soon to drive me to Gwangju. Sorry."

"That's okay. I can manage. I'll make sure to keep the place clean."

"Great. My mom tends to worry, but you seem pretty laid-back for a writer. Maybe because you used to act?"

"I've retired from acting. Now I'm just a high-strung writer," Inkyeong joked, scrunching her face into a frown and making the girl laugh.

Good people raise good people, Inkyeong thought.

On their last day at the center, she'd said to Huisu, "I've really enjoyed my time here, thanks to you. But why are you so nice to me?" Despite the awkwardness of the question, she'd felt compelled to ask.

Huisu paused, then said, "When Bob Dylan was young, his grandmother told him that happiness isn't on the road to anything. She said happiness *is* the road. And that we should be kind because everyone's fighting a hard battle." She added that when she'd first met Inkyeong, for some reason, Bob Dylan had come to mind. For Inkyeong, a Dylan fan herself, this was the perfect answer.

Inkyeong decided to pursue writing the year after Bob Dylan won the Nobel Prize in Literature. He was particularly special to her, because he, a singer, had received a literary award, just as she, Jeong Inkyeong, had transitioned from acting to playwriting. Around the time he received the Nobel, Inkyeong had faced backlash for critiquing a play by a seasoned director. It was hard for people to accept criticism from an actor with no writing experience who'd dared to give a negative review. In response, she submitted a play she had written in her spare time to a literary contest at the year's end, and won, as if to say, "I told you so."

The problem was what followed. After she became a playwright, acting gigs dried up, and her plays struggled to get staged. Some directors felt uncomfortable working with an actor turned playwright, while some stage managers didn't take her plays seriously. Inkyeong felt disrespected and grew anxious. For a while, she was ready to explode at any provocation, and often did, which tarnished her own reputation.

Her decision to leave Daehangno was sealed when she retired from acting. For five years, she had played the lead in a summer production. The role of the twenty-seven-year-old "Runaway Bride Bitna," who flees two days before her wedding, had become Inkyeong's signature part, her calling card in the industry. But the previous spring, the producer informed her that they wouldn't be continuing with her anymore. Noting that her actual age was thirty-seven, he praised her past performances but said it was time to pass the role on to younger actors. That much she could handle. But when he added that he hoped to work with her again in a more "mature role," she had stormed out, slamming the door behind her. Even back in her room, she was still fuming. What did he mean by "mature"? A role for older actors? "You can shove it!" she shouted to herself. She vowed instead to write mature plays.

In the two years since, Inkyeong had managed to complete only a few works. These plays, shoved into folders, had ripened and matured to the point of spoiling, while she spent her days like a ghost wandering Daehangno, helping out in colleagues' productions and drinking too much. Her unexpected contest win had made her a playwright, but her writing skills were still lacking. She wrote and rewrote to refine her craft, but her submissions were always rejected. After countless setbacks, she finally had a play premiere at a friend's theater company that summer. But it was a disaster, not just in box office sales and critical reception but also in her own eyes.

Believing that life was a series of problems to solve, she had prided herself on her problem-solving ability, but even that seemed to have been depleted. The money she'd brought to Seoul a decade ago to chase her acting dreams was long gone, spent on rent, and now she had nothing left. It felt like the curtain had fallen on her dreams. There were no stages for her to perform on, and the ones she tried to create didn't welcome her. Her creativity had dried up, and whatever talent she once had was draining away like a dying phone battery.

Inkyeong unpacked in the room that had been emptied for her and sat at the desk, trying to catch her breath. She had no idea what the next three months had in store for her. Fortunately, Seoul Station was nearby. She told herself that if she couldn't finish anything in three months, she'd head straight to the station and take the first train to Busan. Just then, there was a knock on the door. Huisu's daughter stood with a smile, saying that her boyfriend had arrived to take her to Gwangju.

Left alone, Inkyeong lay down for an early night's sleep. She drifted off almost immediately.

When she woke up, it was midnight. She must have been exhausted. Her T-shirt was damp with sweat, and her stomach was caved in with hunger. Having resolved not to eat any of Huisu's daughter's food, she quickly threw on a jacket and headed out.

Her breath visible in the cold night air, Inkyeong entered the convenience store across the street and was greeted by a deep voice. Behind the counter stood a burly middle-aged man, the type you'd expect to see in theater—like a character actor whose talent outshone his looks. *At least no one would try to rob the store with him around,* she thought as she walked toward the shelves.

The selection was disappointing. Inkyeong's favorite snacks were nowhere in sight, and the refrigerated deli selection wasn't much better. Only gimbap and sandwiches were available, neither of which appealed to her, and the last two lunch boxes looked pretty sad.

Settling for frozen dumplings and beef jerky, Inkyeong headed to the cooler to grab some beer. But none of the "4 Cans/10,000 won" deals included the brands she liked. Sighing, Inkyeong gave up on the deal and picked out two cans of Heineken instead.

"Do you stock only a few kinds of lunch boxes?" she asked.

"Lu-lunch boxes . . . We try not to let too many expire . . ." the man stuttered, as if caught off guard by her question.

This was bad news for Inkyeong, who practically lived on convenience store lunch boxes when deep in her writing. As she gathered her items, she realized she hadn't checked if there was a microwave in the apartment. She scanned the store but didn't see one either. When she asked about it, the man explained it was broken and had been sent out for repairs, apologizing repeatedly in his stuttering way.

"No, it's fine . . . just a bit inconvenient, I guess."

"I guess this place . . . somehow turned into . . . an inconvenience store," the man joked.

Inkyeong was surprised by his honesty and self-deprecating humor. This middle-aged man, calling his own workplace inconvenient—who was he? She looked at him closely. His strong jawline, large nose, half-closed eyes, and broad frame reminded her of a sleepy bear, yet he seemed blissfully unaware of his resemblance as he grinned at her.

"Do you like . . . the Ultimate Feast Lunch Box?"

Inkyeong had no idea how to reply to this random question.

"It's the most popular . . . so it sells out fast . . . Should I save one for you next time?"

"No, no, that's fine."

She hurriedly left the store with her purchases. She heard him call out goodbye in his deep voice. Everything about the store was uncomfortable—from its bad selection to the man's awkward presence. She resolved to come only when the female part-timer who'd let her use the phone was on duty.

The next night, Inkyeong woke up to find it was already 1:00 a.m. She couldn't believe how quickly the day had gone by. After snacking on beef jerky and beer the previous night, she'd worked until morning, turning her room into a workspace. Then, as people headed off to their jobs, she'd wandered past Sookmyung Women's University toward Hyochang Park. Refreshed after five laps around the park, she explored the neighborhood, noting potential walking routes, markets, supermarkets, and restaurants, before returning home to shower. Though tempted to nap, she spent the afternoon researching writing contests and current theater trends. If she wanted to write, she needed motivation, and nothing provided that better than deadlines. But finding no contest that fit her needs, she reminded herself of the personal three-month deadline she had imposed.

In the late afternoon, she treated herself to tofu soup at a nearby restaurant. She missed the free, healthy meals at the Toji Cultural Center, but now that she was back in Seoul, she decided to limit dining out to once a day to save money.

When she returned to the apartment, she turned on an episode of *Breaking Bad*. She turned to this show whenever she felt desperate, as if popping a painkiller. Every time the title appeared on the screen, she muttered, "Cutting Through Bad Luck." Though she later learned that this wasn't the real title, but a mistranslation from the pirated file she'd first acquired, it had left a deep impression on her. The life of the protagonist, Walter White, was like that. To overcome the endless misfortunes he faced, he resorted to manufacturing and selling drugs. Perhaps that was why Inkyeong turned to the series whenever her own future seemed bleak and uncertain. Of course, it was entertaining, and she had much to learn from the writing. Plus, she'd watched it so many times that it helped her fall asleep.

At 1:00 a.m., her stomach growled, reminding her another day had begun. Why hadn't she gone grocery shopping? She really needed to get her days and nights straightened out if she wanted to make the most of her time here, but what she needed right now was food.

As she put on her jacket, she thought about the large, awkward man behind the counter at the convenience store. She considered looking for another store but decided it was better to face the inconvenience of this one than to wander the cold streets at night.

Ding-dong. The store was quiet. She didn't see the man anywhere, and the broken microwave, now apparently repaired, sat in the corner by the window. However, the selection was still disappointing. Inkyeong realized it was probably the result of a vicious cycle: low sales leading to limited stock, which in turn deterred customers. As her hunger gnawed at her, she couldn't help seeing a parallel between the store's plight and her own situation. She headed for the refrigerated deli section.

The lunch box selection was still pathetic, with only two left. They looked suspiciously like the same ones from the day before, but when she looked closer, Inkyeong discovered a different lunch box underneath. She moved the top ones aside and picked up the hidden one, which looked quite appetizing. It boasted twelve different sides with plenty of meat options, making her mouth water. She grabbed the lunch box and approached the counter, but the man was still missing. Was he in the storeroom in the back? How could he leave the store unattended in the middle of the night? *What a truly inconvenient store*, she thought irritably. She was wondering what she should do when a sheet of paper on the counter caught her eye. Scrawled in large, bold letters with a black marker was a message.

CODE BROWN! BRB

Inkyeong couldn't help laughing. An urgent number two? Sure, it could happen, but he should have at least locked the door and placed the note outside. How could he leave it on the counter like this? What if someone noticed there was no one watching the store and decided to make off with the cash and goods? Did he assume the area was so safe he didn't have to worry about theft, or did he not care whether the store got robbed? Even with security cameras, leaving the store unattended could invite crime.

The door chime rang. The man returned, his expression making it clear that he'd rushed back from urgent business. Catching Inkyeong's eye, he muttered something under his breath and scurried back to the counter. She stepped aside to let him pass, shooting him a disapproving look.

"This one . . . is good," he said, as he rang up the lunch box she'd chosen.

When she looked closer, she realized it was the Ultimate Feast Lunch Box he had recommended the day before.

"You found it . . . I hid it for you."

"Pardon me?"

"Last night . . . you were looking for a good lunch box . . . so I tucked it away under the other ones."

Did he expect her to be grateful? Inkyeong didn't know how to respond to this strange gesture of goodwill. After paying, she took the lunch box to the microwave. Since the apartment didn't have one, she had no choice but to use the store's. She removed the plastic wrapper and placed the lunch box in the microwave. When she happened to glance at the man while waiting, he flashed her a thumbs-up. Could he make a person feel any more uncomfortable? Annoyed, she marched toward him.

"Hey, mister, it's not okay to leave the store like that."

"I h-h-had to . . . it was an emergency . . . Look . . ." he stammered, holding up his hastily written note.

"That's exactly why you should lock the door and post the note outside. What if some delinquent walked in and got tempted to steal? Don't you know leaving the store unattended encourages crime? Have you heard of the broken windows theory? If there are broken windows in a neighborhood, theft and other crimes go up. In the same way, leaving your store unattended could invite trouble. You really need to be more responsible."

Inkyeong's lecture was partly due to her habit of calling people out and partly to establish clear boundaries with the man. Men usually backed off after a spiel like that. He listened in silence, then hung his head in shame.

"Actually . . . you're right . . . but can I explain my side?"

"Go ahead."

"I have irritable bowel syndrome . . . it's hard to hold it when I have to go . . . Earlier I was bending down to get tape . . . to stick the note on the door when . . . a little came out . . . I couldn't even stick the note . . . I had to leave it here . . . and rush out without locking the door . . . Then as I was pulling down my pants in the bathroom . . ."

"Stop!"

So he'd had an accident and left in a hurry without locking the door. Inkyeong's stomach turned at the vivid details. She felt like she could almost smell it on him. This was getting more uncomfortable— and infuriating—by the second.

"Okay, okay. Just please be more careful next time."

He bowed in apology, but she ignored him and went back to the microwave to retrieve her meal. As she was about to leave the store, he bowed again and called out, "I'm sorry for the Code Brown today!"

Code Brown? Well, I'm Code Disgusted! Inkyeong was pushing open the door when her patience snapped. She spun around and yelled, "Can you please stop talking about your bathroom emergency when I'm about to eat?"

She was Jeong Inkyeong, the famous "Rage Queen" of Daehangno. The man, dumbfounded by her sudden outburst, stuttered a series of apologies. Inkyeong had enough of his stammering. Muttering under her breath, she stormed out, vowing never to return.

Even after a week at the Cheongpa-dong apartment, Inkyeong hadn't made any progress with her writing. She abandoned the story she'd begun at the Toji Cultural Center and mulled over several new ideas. She wanted to create a drama grounded in reality but not necessarily driven by commercial appeal. She envisioned a vibrant space where characters interacted closely, rubbing shoulders with one another.

A performance that wouldn't alienate the audience but draw them in, one where the audience members could immerse themselves as if they were part of the cast. A work that would keep viewers on the edge of their seats, leaving them to ponder its message long after the curtain had fallen and they had left the theater.

Spending the entire day at her desk only made her more frustrated. With the weather turning colder, she cut back on eating out to save money and began preparing simple meals at home. In the evenings, she sat by the window, sipping tea and watching the neighborhood residents return from work.

Recently, she noticed a middle-aged man who regularly sat at the convenience store's outdoor table around 11:00 p.m. He would polish off a bottle of soju with a bowl of instant noodles before heading home. Dressed in a suit under his parka, with thinning hair that seemed more pitiful from her view above, he mixed his gimbap with his noodles, shoveling mouthfuls and sipping his soju. Despite the cold, this seemed to be his small comfort at the end of the day. Watching him from her window, Inkyeong found herself growing curious about his story and why he chose to drink alone, even on winter nights.

However, tonight was different, because wasn't that the stocky night-shift worker sitting across from him? He was holding a large paper cup and drinking what appeared to be whiskey. Was he drinking on the job now? Was that why he stuttered when he spoke—because he was drunk? It was none of her business, yet she found his behavior truly baffling. Then she saw it wasn't alcohol he was pouring into the cup but something else. Judging by the plastic bottle, it looked like barley tea, or maybe green tea or detox tea. Inkyeong started watching them more closely.

The two continued to share the brownish drink, chatting away, when suddenly the office worker snapped something at the man and stormed off. The store worker just shrugged, cleaned up the table, and went back inside. Inkyeong's curiosity was piqued. She threw on her parka and left the apartment for the first time in days.

"Do you know the man who just left?" she asked, striding into the store.

Her abrupt appearance and question seemed to take the store worker off guard.

"H-he's a regular here."

"What does he do?"

"I'm not sure . . . But he really likes So-So-So."

"So-So-So?"

"Somyeon noodles, soboro gimbap, and soju . . . That's what he always gets."

"What did he say to you just now? He seemed pretty upset."

"Oh, that . . . I told him to stop drinking . . . and try something else instead . . . He didn't like that, I guess."

"What did you tell him to try?"

"This."

As if it were no big deal, the man held up the plastic bottle next to him. It was corn silk tea.

"Huh? Why that?"

"It's good for quitting drinking . . . Because of this . . . I was able to quit too."

Inkyeong didn't know what to say. This man was even odder than she'd thought. If she'd found him off-putting before, she was now intrigued. Suggesting corn silk tea to a regular instead of alcohol seemed like a bad business move. Her curiosity grew.

"Excuse me, but what line of work were you in before this?"

"Did you come . . . just to ask me that?" He gestured toward the products on the shelf.

Maybe he's not such a bad businessman after all, the sly dog.

Inkyeong gave a nod and got a bowl of instant somyeon, a soboro triangle gimbap, a bottle of soju, as well as a bottle of corn silk tea, then placed them on the counter. She asked him the same question again, but he just cocked his head without answering.

"Were you in a gang or something?"

"N-no."

"Then are you in rehab after getting out of prison?"

"No . . . I'm not that kind of person."

"Are you supporting a family overseas, then?"

"No."

"Ah, so you're retired! I hear a lot of people are taking early retirement these days, with all the voluntary packages. Right?"

He shook his head, looking uncomfortable, and handed her a plastic bag with her items. Instead of taking it, Inkyeong fixed him with a stare, determined to get to the bottom of his story.

"Come on, what's your deal? I'm genuinely curious."

"I-I was homeless."

"Huh? Like one of the people at Seoul Station?"

"Yes."

"And before that?"

"I don't remember . . . I drank too much, so I got dementia."

"How long were you homeless?"

"I don't . . . remember that either."

"Then how did you end up working here? How did you get this job?"

"The boss . . . told me to stop staying out in the cold at Seoul Station . . . and spend the winter here . . . so I started working here."

"Wow! Just wow!" Inkyeong blurted, unable to contain her fascination.

She pressed him again about his memory—if he really remembered nothing—and he admitted that while it felt like something was on the verge of coming back, he couldn't quite grasp it. Inkyeong suggested that talking more might jog his memory. Before she knew it, she found herself offering to come back for more chats. The man hesitated but reluctantly agreed in the end. She asked his name once more.

Back in her room, Inkyeong sang to herself as she ate her So-So-So. "My name's Dokgo, that's all I know. Don't know my first name or my last name." Discovering such an unusual character, so different from who she'd originally thought he was, made the soju taste sweeter. The So-So-So combo, perfect for a late-night snack or a solo drink, was a nice change. The corn silk tea seemed a bit out of place, but the fact that the man was using it to quit drinking made it feel meaningful. Inkyeong resolved to keep watching him.

Since she wasn't having any luck changing her reversed sleep schedule, Inkyeong decided to make the most of it. She woke up in the middle of the night and, as if going to work, went to the convenience store, where she ate an Ultimate Feast Lunch Box while chatting with Dokgo. He turned out to be much smarter and more perceptive than she'd expected. After several days, Inkyeong began bringing a notebook to jot down notes from their conversations. This unexpected fieldwork gave her the courage to believe she could write again.

It appeared that Dokgo had lost parts of his memories to alcohol-related dementia and psychological trauma. Having read extensively about psychology in her quest to become a writer, Inkyeong was particularly interested in emotional wounds. She understood that a person's future was often shaped by the traumas of their past, and what they sought to protect often dictated their future. Dokgo had shut himself off from his past, but he was on the path to healing, and through his interactions with others, he was slowly finding the courage and strength to confront his wounds.

The drive to face and overcome personal traumas shaped a person's motivations and defined their character. To reveal a character, one simply needed to show the path they chose at life's crossroads. With the help of the convenience store owner, Dokgo had reentered society and was working to address his past.

"One thing I know for sure ; . . . I wasn't like this before. I don't think I interacted with people much. Because I don't have a lot of warm memories."

"Warm memories? What do you mean?"

"Talking openly . . . like this . . ."

"Really? But you seem to talk just fine with people, like that customer who gets the So-So-So."

"That's what I mean . . . I think working here, dealing with customers . . . made me more approachable. Pretending to be nice, even when you don't mean it, actually makes you nicer."

"That's good. You mind if I write that down?" Inkyeong asked, copying Dokgo's words into her notebook.

"You're already writing it down . . ."

"No, I mean for my play. I told you I'm a playwright."

"Ah, right. You said you write plays. So . . . am I going to be in it?"

"I'm not sure yet. It's all sketches for now . . . But you've been a huge help. I was about to give up on writing, but you've given me inspiration."

"I've been helpful? That's nice to hear. So . . . you need anything else while you're here?"

"Were you in sales before?" Inkyeong asked, chuckling.

She brought four cans of beer and a sandwich to the counter. With a salesman's grin, Dokgo cheerfully rang up her items. This relationship between muse and writer was proving to be quite beneficial.

Meaningless year-end greetings and well-wishes flooded Inkyeong's phone. She ignored the group messages, and among the missed calls there were only a few names she was happy to see. She logged on to Facebook for the first time in a while, only to find it filled with people she found more annoying than interesting. Inkyeong had to admit that her dwindling social connections were mostly her own doing. Just then, her phone rang, as if sensing her loneliness. But the caller ID showed it was Mr. Kim, the head of Theater Q—the producer who'd told her almost two years ago that she was too old to keep playing a twentysomething. He had once been a key supporter of her career, but they hadn't exchanged a single message in close to two years.

She rose from her desk and walked over to the chair by the window, her heart trembling as much as the vibrating phone in her hand. Ignoring the call would likely sever her connection with Mr. Kim. The phone kept vibrating. She suddenly recalled how she had urged Dokgo to face his trauma a few days ago. Realizing she, too, needed to confront her own issues, she pressed the button.

Mr. Kim asked how she was doing, casually mentioning that she had come to mind because it was the end of the year.

"And I didn't come to mind last year?" she snapped.

He smoothly explained he hadn't called the year before because he assumed she wouldn't answer, but this year he thought enough time had passed that she wouldn't hold a grudge. His words dissolved the last of Inkyeong's bitterness.

"I'm sure you didn't call just to check in. So what's up?"

"Impatient as ever, I see," he said, chuckling. He then asked if she'd be willing to adapt a novel into a play. An adaptation . . . Her next project could very well be her last, and she didn't want it to be an adaptation. Sensing her hesitation, Mr. Kim urged her to take the job.

"At least read the novel if you're not sure. It was published this summer. It's fun and easy to get into, with a lot of dialogue. It's perfect for theater, actually. What I'm saying is, it won't be hard to adapt."

"No, I can't read it. If I do, I might want to work on it."

"Hey, I'm reaching out after a long time . . . If you don't at least hear me out, you're going to hurt my feelings."

"Mr. Kim, I might be giving up writing for good. If I'm going to do one last project, I want it to be something of my own."

"You quit acting and now you're quitting writing too?"

"I'm serious. I've been locked away brainstorming for the past four months."

"So, got any solid ideas? Or have you been daydreaming the whole time?"

Daydreaming? Inkyeong took a gulp of her corn silk tea, a bit stung by the comment. "I've finished brainstorming, thank you very much. I just need to write it now."

"Oh yeah? Let's hear it."

"Don't you know talking about something too early could jinx it? Forget it."

"You've got me curious now. Come on, spill the beans. If it's good, we'll go with your play instead of the adaptation."

She'd only mentioned she was working on her own project, yet she hadn't really outlined anything. She was still trying to find the story. Unsure of what to say next, she glanced out at the convenience store below.

"If you're hesitating to share, maybe there's nothing there. Let's put that on hold and focus on this adaptation. We've already got the funding. I can get you an advance right away—"

"It's about a convenience store."

"A convenience store?"

"Yeah. It's set in a convenience store, full of all kinds of characters from every walk of life. The lead is this strange night-shift worker."

"Hmm . . ."

"He's a middle-aged man who's lost his memories to alcohol-related dementia. Customers speculate about his backstory, saying he used to be a gangster, an ex-convict, a North Korean defector, an early retiree, even an alien! But the man doesn't care what they think and recommends odd products to them . . . but somehow, his weird recommendations solve their problems."

"That sounds like *Midnight Diner*."

"*Midnight Diner*? Sure, that's a great show, but the core of my story is uncovering who the night worker really is. We'll have flash-backs, find out why he's at the convenience store, and why he spends all night waiting."

"He's probably waiting for a delivery."

"Come on, I'm serious. I'm thinking of giving it the same tone and feel as *Waiting for Godot*. Like Vladimir and Estragon, this worker chats with a drunk customer every night. There'll be a lot of dialogue. And they'll have So-So-So while they talk too."

"So-So-So? What's that—a game?"

"No, it's a convenience store thing, like a marketing combo. Basically, somyeon noodles, soboro gimbap, and soju—So-So-So."

"That's clever. We could get some product placement going. Maybe even have the audience come up and try it."

"Exactly. Get the audience involved, give out some freebies, have them post on Instagram, and boom, brand sponsorship cash. So-

So-So is what the store owner recommends to his regulars. It's their way to unwind after a long day, and they drive most of the dialogue. Then there's this cranky female writer in the neighborhood. She's a bit of a pain in the ass, really. Being a writer, she works at night, so she keeps bumping into the night-shift guy, and they end up talking . . ."

"Sounds like someone I know."

"Nah, and she hates this convenience store. Thinks the guy looks shady and the selection is terrible. But it's winter, it's cold, and she doesn't want to go far to buy food in the middle of the night, so she keeps going back. Honestly, this place couldn't be more inconvenient."

"All right."

"What?"

"Let's do it, you and me."

"Really? But I haven't even written it yet."

"Well, it sounds like you've got it all figured out in your head. Let's stage it next year. I guarantee this won't be your last piece. After this, you'll have more stories to write."

"Do you really think so?"

"Absolutely."

"This is weird . . . I was at the end of my rope here, and it's uncanny you're agreeing to it so easily. I haven't even put a word on paper."

"Just stop by with the title tomorrow. You know how it works. Once the contract is signed, the writing follows."

"Mr. Kim."

"What?"

"Thank you. Truly."

"I'm not an idiot. The concept is solid. You'll be great."

"Well, I *am* a great writer, after all," she said, laughing.

"I take back my compliment. Jeez. Anyway, what's the title?"

"The title?"

"Yeah, for your play."

"Um . . . it's set in a convenience store, but it's anything but convenient . . . so it's called *The Inconvenient . . . The Inconvenience Store!*"

Right after hanging up, Inkyeong opened Word on her laptop and began typing furiously. She wrote the title, skipped a few lines, and started what could be her last work. Her fingers flew across the keys. Some writing is just typing. If you've spent enough time nurturing a cluster of ideas, the slightest touch will make them burst. At that point, your job as a writer is to become a typist, diligently pressing the keys. If your fingers can't keep up with your racing thoughts, you're on the right track.

As she typed, Inkyeong recited the dialogue out loud, as if performing each line. Her left and right hands seemed to be in conversation with each other. It was as if her long-dormant writing talent had been unleashed, and she wrote without stopping. She'd started in the evening, but soon it was past midnight, and as the winter night deepened, so did the intensity of her words.

By dawn, the only lights on in the neighborhood were at Dokgo's convenience store and her studio.

6

Four Cans for 10,000 Won

Minsik thought about his bad luck. His life had always been un-lucky, but he tried to pinpoint exactly when his string of bad luck had taken hold and refused to let go. Could it have been in elementary school, when he couldn't join the baseball team? Despite being big and athletic enough that the coach offered him a spot on the team, his parents pushed him into academics instead. That moment seemed to mark the beginning of his unlucky streak. Why had they insisted on him studying and becoming like everyone else, instead of letting him chase his passions? Didn't they know that everyone had their own talents and interests? They expected Minsik to be like them and his sister, who'd always done well in school.

The next bit of bad luck probably came when Minsik ended up going to a regional campus. His parents had dreamed of him attending their prestigious alma mater in Seoul, but with Minsik's grades, that was impossible, so they'd settled for the next best thing—the university's regional campus. They probably bragged to their friends that he was going to their old school, but he focused his energies on drinking, playing pool and StarCraft, and joining the campus baseball club. He had a lot of fun. Somehow, he managed to graduate, but job hunting was brutal due to the stigma of attending a regional campus, which crushed his pride and motivation.

His third stroke of bad luck came from tasting success too early. Unlike his parents, who'd led stable lives as a civil servant and a teacher, or his sister, who'd carved out a respectable career that everyone envied, Minsik had to fight tooth and nail to survive. He wasn't the sharpest or most educated, but he was armed with a healthy body and a smooth tongue, and he chased whatever paid well. Money was his all-in-one solution, the only way he could prove himself to his family. If he could get money, he figured everything would fall into place. It was the one thing that could define him.

Minsik wasn't picky about how he earned his money, even if it meant walking a fine line between what was legal and what wasn't. He moved forward without hesitation or remorse. Through his ventures, he amassed enough wealth to buy a condo in his own name and a fancy foreign car before turning thirty. His success meant that his parents, his sister, and even his stuck-up brother-in-law couldn't dictate his life. He loved the power that wealth gave him. Just a bit more, he thought, and he'd see them groveling. A generous allowance for his recently retired father and a sizable church donation for his mother would surely dazzle them, while his sister and brother-in-law would come crawling for an investment in their new clinic. Success was just around the corner, but that was precisely the problem. His ambition led him to grow his business too quickly, and soon the consequences caught up with him.

The fourth stroke of bad luck was particularly painful: meeting his (now ex) wife. While trying to launch a new business and stage a comeback, he met a beautiful woman who was every bit the "businessperson" he was. He never thought he would fall for someone so quickly, but within six months, he was head over heels, pouring everything he had into the relationship. Some might have called it love, but in retrospect, he saw it as a moment of insanity. They rushed into marriage, and after two years of constantly trying to outdo each other, he was outplayed by his shrewder ex-wife, who walked away with his last asset: the condo. Only then did their marriage end. Now, two years after the divorce, he realized that their relationship had been as much a disaster for her as it was for him. Their decision to split, before something even worse happened, was thanks to their knack for timing, honed through their business experience, but his bad luck didn't stop there.

Next up was Bitcoin. Minsik was convinced it would be his golden ticket, but it turned out to be a big mistake. For him, Bitcoin became a forbidden fruit, a money-eating monster.

After this fifth disaster, Minsik hit rock bottom and was left with no choice but to crawl back to his mother's place in Cheongpa-dong. There, he discovered she had opened a convenience store with the money left behind by his father, who had passed away a few years earlier—an inheritance that surely included his share. His mother and sister had turned his portion into a business without even consulting him. Not that Minsik had been thinking clearly at the time; he'd been too consumed by his divorce and failing investments. Besides, he had cut off contact with his family. Feeling cheated, he confronted his mom one night while drunk, demanding his share of the money, which led to a massive fight and him storming out. From that point on, he had been bouncing from one friend's place to another.

His thoughts stopped there. Dwelling on the smaller misfortunes that followed seemed pointless. What he needed now was capital for a new venture, and that capital was tied up in his mother's convenience store—the store she'd opened with *his* money and without his consent. He planned to reclaim his share, jump-start his business, and begin raking in the cash again. Once he did that, opening a couple of new convenience stores for his mom would be easy. Then, he could finally tell off the friend who kept grumbling about Minsik overstaying his welcome, constantly asking when he planned to leave.

Minsik was supposed to meet Giyong today, a wannabe rapper who insisted on being called Gi-Dragon, after G-Dragon. Giyong's over-the-top antics could be annoying, but he was smart. For the past several years, he had sought Giyong's opinion on major decisions. Giyong often offered perspectives that Minsik hadn't considered and had a knack for prompting Minsik to rethink his choices. Although following his advice didn't always guarantee success, it helped steer Minsik away from pitfalls. "By the time you hear something is profitable, it's already too late to invest. Get out before you're completely cleaned out," Giyong had once told him. Thanks to Giyong, Minsik had narrowly escaped falling even deeper into the Bitcoin trap. It was also Giyong who advised him to pull out of the solar power project.

When a senior colleague had proposed working together on that project, Minsik felt like the sun was finally shining on his life again, and his whole body had tingled with excitement. The project attracted many investors, bolstered by government policies favoring renewable energy over nuclear power. It had seemed like a great opportunity to get in on early. But after a few months, Minsik started to feel uneasy, unable to shake the thought that the venture might be a scam, essentially selling worthless land disguised as solar power investment. This time, too, after a phone call with Giyong, Minsik managed to exit the project just in time.

That executive went berserk when Minsik backed out, warning him to watch his back. However, in a twist of irony, that same jerk was nabbed by the cops one night and was now getting his meals courtesy of the Ministry of Justice. Without Giyong's heads-up, Minsik might have ended up with a similar fate, adding a prison chapter to his already tumultuous career. With all that in mind, when Giyong said he had a new business idea, Minsik trusted him enough to immediately borrow a friend's down parka and brave the cold to meet him in Itaewon.

Gyeongnidan Street at the start of the new year was eerily quiet, a stark contrast to its once-bustling days. It now felt abandoned. As often happens, when a commercial area becomes popular, landlords get greedy and hike up the rent, forcing many stores to close and subsequently draining the life from the neighborhood. Gyeongnidan Street seemed destined to fade away, leaving behind similar-sounding hot spots like Mangridan Street, Songridan Street, and Hwangridan Street. Minsik was confused why Giyong, of all people, wanted to meet in a ghost town.

When he arrived at the address Giyong had given him, Minsik found a small pub on the desolate street and parked his car right in front.

"Hey, bro, I told you not to bring your car," Giyong said as soon as Minsik stepped inside.

"You expect me to freeze my ass off on the bus?"

"There's something called a taxi, you know."

"I've got my car. Why the hell should I take a taxi?"

"There's a reason I told you not to bring it. We have to drink today."

"Here? You know I don't like beer, right?"

Giyong ignored him and headed to the bar, uninterested in Minsik's protests. Minsik flopped down on a metal chair, resting his arms on the tiny table while taking in his surroundings. Under the dim lights, the air vibrated with the loud strains of an electric guitar, and Western antiques, clearly catering to the tastes of American soldiers who once frequented the area, were scattered around the pub. At the back, a tacky banner declared "Drink Beer, Save Water." The place was so cold he could see his breath—probably a tactic to encourage more drinking.

Minsik was irritated. He viewed beer as something to mix with soju or whiskey and couldn't believe Giyong had brought him to a pub. His doubts about any business proposal Giyong might pitch deepened. Oblivious to Minsik's irritation, Giyong returned to the table carrying what the long-haired bartender had handed him. It looked like a wooden board with holes, each holding a small glass slightly bigger than a soju shot glass. The drinks ranged in color from dark amber to black. The one that looked like soy sauce was probably stout, while the amber one reminded Minsik of cognac.

"These are supposed to be beer?"

"Try it."

Giyong grinned and gestured for him to drink. Minsik was already annoyed at the thought of drinking beer from a soju glass, but he grabbed the amber-colored one and downed it in one gulp, embracing the spirit of free alcohol.

The flavor was full and bold, with an intense aroma and a unique bitter aftertaste that could easily be mistaken for cognac or whiskey. It was a completely new experience for Minsik, far from the bland beers he was used to. It reminded him more of a well-crafted whiskey bomb.

Without another word, Minsik picked up the glass with the darker amber liquid and drank. *Oh!* This one had an even richer flavor, with a surprising blend of bitterness and hops. Next, he polished off a yellowish beer with lots of foam. It was similar to the Hoegaarden he'd tried once, but this one was drier and more robust. Finally, Minsik sniffed the stout before gulping it down. *What was this creaminess?* It was rich and velvety, like drinking a dessert in liquid form.

"What kind of beer is this?"

"It's good, right?"

"Forget about the soju glasses. Fill up a proper glass and bring it to me."

"Which one?"

"The darkest one."

Giyong took the wooden board and soon returned with two tall glasses of fresh beer. After clinking them together, Minsik took a sip. The bitter, refreshing taste outdid any whiskey bomb, even those made with thirty-year-old Ballantine's. The flavor was a revelation. He'd long dismissed beer as too bland and filling—where had this been all his life?

"It's an ale. It's what they drink in Europe."

"Ale? So, what's Cass then? The one everyone drinks here?"

"That's a lager. It says so on the can."

"Really? I always thought that word next to Cass was *laser*."

"Wow, your English is something else, man. Lagers are more common here and in the U.S., but in Europe, it's all about ales. They've been catching on in Gyeongnidan and Itaewon for the past few years. Hipsters are all over them," Giyong said.

"But this could appeal to an older crowd too. It's totally my style. The flavor's rich, and honestly, it smells better than some cognacs ... Hey, what if we supplied this to room salons?"

"Why are you bringing room salons into this? Those places have their own distributors, and they're shady as hell. Let's keep it clean and simple."

"Business is all about taking opportunities. What's clean and simple about that?"

"I'm saying let's not complicate things. The ale scene is growing, and thanks to new laws, people can open small breweries to make craft beer."

"Really?" asked Minsik.

"Yeah. For two to three hundred million won, you could set up a brewery somewhere with a good water supply, like on the outskirts of Gyeonggi-do, say Gapyeong or Cheongpyeong. Imagine if we brewed it there and sold it. You were talking about wanting a simpler life, maybe running a bar. Why not own a brewery instead? If we make beer this good, bars will be lining up for it. It could be huge!"

"So, this beer's from one of those craft breweries?"

"Exactly."

"Who made it?"

Just then, the savory smell of frying oil wafted through the air and the long-haired bartender approached with a platter of chicken wings and fries. Giyong gestured toward the bartender as he set down the food, introducing him to Minsik like he was presenting a new product. The bartender shot Minsik a friendly smile and joined them at the table.

"This guy's brother-in-law, Steve, he's a brewmaster. *Brew* as in beer, and *master* as in, well . . . a master. Basically a chef, but for beer. Steve's from Portland and runs a small brewery."

Seeing Minsik's confusion, the bartender elaborated. Four years ago, Steve, who'd been making the hippest beer in Portland—often considered the hippest city in America—fell for the bartender's sister, who was studying in the States, and ended up visiting Korea. After trying the local beer, Steve became convinced that authentic craft beer could be a hit in Korea. Two years later, the couple got married, moved to Korea, and started the brewery in Paju. Steve runs it, while the bartender supplies bars, including this one, with his brother-in-law's craft beer.

"But if ale's more a European thing, why are we talking about America?"

"Man, it's a global world now. Don't you know the U.S. is great at taking European trends and blowing them up? Anyway, Steve's brewery is doing so well they're looking to expand. They need a new business partner, and that's where we come in."

"Hmm . . . this feels a bit random. But a brewery owner, huh? I gotta admit, it's kinda weird to think about a legit opportunity after all this time. If it's as successful as you say, there must be plenty of investors lined up. Why would Steve want to work with us?"

"At least ask the right questions."

"But that's what you told me during the solar project fiasco. You said I always show up late to the party."

"Hey, this time it's all me. Steve's super picky about who he works with, but I cracked him up with my Konglish. Told him straight up I'm someone he can trust. Steve even told this guy here," Giyong said, gesturing to the bartender, "that most Koreans are iffy, but Gi-Dragon's solid. For Steve, it's all about relationships, especially when you're thinking to expand, and he said he can trust me."

Giyong glanced at the bartender, who flashed a thumbs-up. The bartender added that his brother-in-law doesn't normally warm up to people, but for some reason, he took a real liking to Giyong. Minsik knew Giyong was a funny guy, but it was intriguing—and a bit suspicious—that he'd charmed an American enough to score this kind of opportunity. And, of course, Americans could be con artists too.

Sensing Minsik's skepticism, the bartender brought over a plain 500-milliliter can of beer, cracked it open, and poured it into a fresh glass. Once again, Minsik couldn't help marveling at the taste.

"We're gonna do cans too. That's part of the expansion plan."

Minsik found himself nodding along.

"Bro, Steve's beer will be in convenience stores and supermarkets soon. Other breweries have already made it into retail. We need to move fast. With our taste and your experience in distribution, we just have to jump in and start selling."

Minsik took another sip, deep in thought. The blend of sweet malt and bitter hops brought back memories of past successes. What Giyong said next sealed the deal.

"Remember this summer when all the Japanese beers disappeared from shelves? Your mom owns a convenience store, right? Go take a look. Asahi, Kirin, Sapporo—they used to be four cans at ten thousand won, but now they're all gone. The boycott's our opportunity. Think about it. What's gonna fill that void? Cass? Hite? Nah, Steve's ale will."

"The boycott of Japanese products . . . you think it'll last?" Minsik asked, voicing his last bit of doubt.

Clearly annoyed, Giyong gulped down his beer and slammed the glass on the table.

"Man, have you forgotten what country we live in? We don't need an independence movement anymore, but boycotts? We're all over that. This is Korea. Dae-han-min-guk! We're in a trade war! Think about the baseball and soccer rivalries with Japan. The whole 'Prepare for the worst if we lose'? Nobody's drinking Japanese beer now. Your patriotism is looking a little weak, my friend."

"Why drag patriotism into this? I'm doing my part. I haven't smoked Mevius in ages."

"So, you in or out? I know you've been lying low. I'm offering you a chance to bounce back, but you gotta be ready to step up. You know I'm discerning, right? I was never on board with any of your 'great opportunities,' but I'm all in on this. Wow, I never thought I'd see Kang Minsik this unsure."

Minsik raised his glass instead of replying. The bartender stood up and refilled it right away. Minsik took a thoughtful sip of the amber ale, savoring it. He set his glass down and playfully smacked Giyong on the back of his head, matching his scowl.

"How much do I need to put in?"

Minsik called a service to have a driver take his car to Cheongpa-dong. Once they arrived , he lingered outside his mother's apartment, feeling awkward about the sudden drop-in. More importantly, he needed a solid pitch. Convincing his sober mom to try the ale didn't seem like the right approach either. Just then, an idea struck him, and he let out a quiet "Aha!" before setting off in a new direction.

The convenience store—half of which was rightfully his. Giyong had mentioned ales were already on store shelves. Wouldn't ale from his mother's store clearly demonstrate this product's potential?

It was past eleven, and the store was completely empty. The lonely Christmas tree by the door, still not taken down, blinked depressingly. Wearing a sour expression, Minsik opened the door and walked in.

"Hello!"

A deep voice greeted him as he made his way toward the beer cooler. It seemed the night-shift worker had changed, from one with a round face to another with a square one. He recalled how his mom had asked him two months ago to cover nights at the store until she found a replacement. The request had been ludicrous, stirring up the old anger of being seen as just another body to fill a shift. He felt a twinge of guilt, wondering if maybe he should have helped out and then pushed for a bigger share of the store. But living like these middle-aged losers, pushed to the edges of society, wasn't an option for him. Now in his forties, Minsik considered himself to be in the prime of his life. Once you start falling behind, you go down fast. He wanted to establish himself as a brewery or bar owner and start the second act of his life.

Standing in front of the beer fridge, Minsik hesitated, unsure
what to get. The space once filled with Japanese beers was now
stocked with various international ones, and the local brews Giyong
had mentioned were nowhere to be seen. He opened the door and
examined the lineup, finally spotting two cans with tacky Korean
labels: Beer Mountain Sobaeksan and Beer Mountain Taebaeksan,
labeled as pale ale and golden ale. Minsik grabbed a can of each,
along with two cans of Tsingtao for comparison, and walked to the
counter.

Up close, the square-faced cashier was a big guy. Minsik stared at
him, thinking he looked like a bear. A guy like him could probably
scare off any thieves at night. Watching him fumble with the bar
code scanner, Minsik couldn't help smirking.

"Hey, do you sell a lot of these local beers?" Minsik asked, holding up the can of Sobaeksan.

"Um . . . not really."

"Ever tried it? How's it taste?"

The man finished ringing up the beer and looked at Minsik. "I . . .
don't drink . . . so I wouldn't know."

Really? Minsik thought, amused. *You sure look like the beer-
loving type.* He wondered if the worker was testing him.

"Oh yeah? You look like you'd enjoy a beer, but okay."

"That'll be fourteen thousand won."

"Isn't it ten thousand won for four cans?"

"That deal . . . doesn't apply . . . not to these local beers . . ."

"What? Maybe they'd sell better if they were four for ten thousand."

"I . . . wouldn't know about that."

"Right, you don't make those decisions. Just bag them up, please."

But the man stood there, staring. What was his problem? Did
Minsik's comment rub him the wrong way? Would you believe the

nerve of this part-timer? But when the man didn't budge, Minsik sensed something was up. The guy's square jaw and piercing gaze were a bit intimidating, but Minsik wasn't about to back down.

"Are you going to bag these or what?"

"You need to pay first."

That's when it hit Minsik—he hadn't mentioned who he was. "Oh, right, I forgot to let you know. I'm the store owner's son. Just put them on our tab."

But the man kept staring. Minsik realized he needed to take control of the situation by being the first to drop the polite speech.

"What's the holdup here?" Minsik snapped.

Still, the man didn't move.

"You know the granny who runs this place? I'm her son, get it?"

"Then . . . prove it."

"Excuse me?"

"Show me proof . . . that you're her son."

"Did you just talk down to me?"

"Yup . . . just like you did."

"Listen, you idiot. Haven't you seen the owner? I look just like her. The eyes, the hawk nose."

"Not . . . really. You don't . . . look alike," he said slowly, his tone mocking.

Minsik was stunned, even a little scared by the intense way the man was staring at him. Minsik's confidence wavered slightly, but he decided to unleash the anger building inside him.

"You shithead! Will firing you help prove I'm her son? I'm going to tell my mom . . . No, scratch that, this store's mine! Understand? I could fire you this instant. Got that?"

"You can't . . . fire me."

"What the hell? Are you out of your mind?"

"If you fire me . . . who's going to cover the night shift?"

"I'll find someone else. There are plenty of people out there."

"You can't . . . fire me . . . Finding someone to work nights . . . isn't easy . . . It's not like you're going to do it yourself . . . Plus, the owner . . . she's sick."

"What?"

"You heard me . . . She said she had a son . . . who doesn't give a damn . . . even though she's sick."

"She said that?"

"You didn't know? Figures . . . She's been going to the hospital . . . for the past few days."

"What?"

"Your mother's sick . . . And instead of looking after her . . . here you are, trying to fire me . . . What about the night shift then? . . . You're going to make her do it again? You call yourself . . . family?"

Thud. Something inside Minsik plummeted. A sharp pain shot through him, pulling him back to reality. He'd had no idea that his mom was sick or that she'd said those things about him to someone else. The man's words, delivered so methodically, as if reading a verdict, weighed heavily on Minsik.

"If she's really your mother . . . this isn't how . . . you should treat her."

"Uh . . . Uhh . . ."

"Since you can't prove you're her son . . . I can't let you take the beer . . . or the bag."

The man's blunt words struck Minsik's flushed face like a one-two punch.

"Fuck it. I don't want them anymore," Minsik blurted, storming out of the store.

But it wasn't the man's size that chased him away. It was his own shame.

Minsik hurried to his mom's apartment, punched in the door pass-code, and went inside. The only light illuminating the dark interior came from the television screen, and his mom was curled up on the couch, sleeping despite the lively music from the TV show.

Letting out a sigh, he flicked on the living-room lights and gently shook her awake. She opened her eyes, looked up at him groggily, and struggled to sit up.

"What's going on? What are you doing here?"

"Are you sick? I rushed over as soon as I heard."

"It's you I've been worried about. Where have you been all this time?"

"Really? You're going to start nagging the second you see me? I was staying at a friend's place. Are you okay?"

"It's just the flu. And some body aches."

"I told you to get the flu shot. It's free for seniors at the clinic."

Mrs. Yeom let out a groan and shuffled to the kitchen. Minsik hovered by her side, trying to break the awkward silence.

"Mom, it's freezing in here. No wonder you're sick. Turn up the heat."

"Who's nagging now? It's fine. Got warmer after you came. Guess you do bring some warmth after all."

"Wow, Mom. I honestly don't know how your students survived your sarcasm."

"Want some tea?"

"Sure."

Minsik took a seat at the dining table and peeled off his socks. Mrs. Yeom brought over two cups of the barley tea she'd boiled earlier and sat down, clucking her tongue at the sight of his socks tossed on the floor.

They sipped their tea in silence, feeling the stillness of the night deepen as midnight approached. Minsik didn't know where to start. He'd planned to bring up the beer business using the ales he brought over from the store, but the buffoon had derailed his plans. Where had the nutjob come from? Just thinking about him made Minsik's blood start boiling again.

"What's the matter with you?" Mrs. Yeom asked, noticing the scowl on Minsik's face.

"Mom, I just stopped by the store. Who's the criminal-looking dude?"

"Oh, you mean Mr. Dokgo? He's been covering the night shift."

"What a piece of work—so rude and full of himself."

"Well, it's not like he's working at some fancy department store where manners are everything."

"Still, his customer service is terrible. I didn't tell him who I was at first, but when I tried to put something on the family tab, he actually asked for proof I was your son."

Mrs. Yeom chuckled, and Minsik, irritated, took a gulp of his barley tea.

"He's thorough. He's just doing his job."

"It's insulting, Mom. Can we fire him?"

"Should we?"

"Yeah. I can't stand him. He's a lawsuit waiting to happen. I let it slide, but what if he pulls that on a drunk customer? We'd be in deep trouble. We might have to pay compensation."

"He's great with drunk customers. Plus, he's a hit with the neighborhood grandmas who come in the morning. Our sales have gone up since he started."

"How much can sales from a tiny store go up? Forget about firing him, maybe we should just sell the store."

"No."

"Why not?"

"If I close the store, Mrs. Oh and Mr. Dokgo will lose their jobs. They rely on this for their livelihood."

"Are you Mother Teresa now? Does going to church mean you have to save everyone?"

"It's not just because I'm a Christian. It's about doing what's right. As a boss, you have a responsibility to your employees."

"You call running a convenience store being a boss?"

"That attitude, son, is exactly why you're not one and keep getting stuck in these dead-end jobs. Understand?"

"Ah, not this lecture again . . . We can talk about selling the store later, but first things first. Let's get rid of that guy."

"No."

"Why not?"

"It's hard to find someone to work nights. But if you're willing to work those hours, I'll consider firing him."

"Why are you so eager to stick your son with these menial jobs? Is that what you want for me—to work at a convenience store?"

"Work is work. With the wage hike these days, working the night shift can net you over two million won a month."

"Ugh, I knew I should have kept my mouth shut. Fine, let him stay."

Minsik downed his tea, but the sting of their conversation kept his anger simmering. He couldn't stand the idea of walking away defeated, not securing any cash for his plans, and also getting reamed out by his mom. Deciding to at least pitch his idea, Minsik opened the fridge for some cold water, but what was this?

Minsik stared at the last thing he expected to see in his mother's fridge: cans of the beer he'd intended to bring back from the store, the exact beer he'd planned to pitch as part of his business idea. He

grabbed a can of Beer Mountain Sobaeksan and returned to the table. His mom looked surprised for a second but quickly played it
cool.

Minsik cracked open the can and poured the beer into his empty
glass. The strong aroma of the ale tickled his nose—this was the
perfect moment to win her over. He took a big gulp. *Aah*. It wasn't
as good as Steve's brew, but it was definitely richer than the average
beer.

"Ah, this is good. I never thought you'd have something like this
in your fridge."

"Headquarters recommended it as a new product. Not bad,
right?"

"Wait, you actually drank it? Since when do you drink?"

"Don't go blabbing about it. It's for work. I have to know what
we're selling."

"Then you're going to start trying all the cigarettes too? Aren't
you being a little too lax, Mom? Haha."

Mrs. Yeom frowned at his teasing, finished her barley tea, and set
her glass down.

"That's enough. Pour me some."

Yes! Doing a victory dance inside, he carefully poured his mom a
glass, making sure the foam was just right.

For the next hour, they drank together, polishing off all four cans
from the fridge. It was the first time Minsik had ever had a real
drink with his mom, face-to-face. He found it odd—not just that
she drank, but that they were having a genuine conversation. For
the past few years, Minsik had always asked her for something, and
she'd always said no, whatever it was. That's why their conversations kept getting cut short. But now, with both of them slightly
buzzed, Minsik found himself spilling all kinds of stories to her.

They chuckled over tales of his stubborn dad and poked fun at his goody-two-shoes brother-in-law. He also caught up on the latest gossip from his mom's church, which he'd once attended, and heard stories about the neighbors, including the latest drama over noise complaints. His mom seemed starved for conversation, talking like someone who had just received the gift of tongues. He was fascinated to hear her thoughts about the people around them. They saw exactly eye to eye on his dad, sister, and brother-in-law, but when it came to the church crowd and the neighbors, they had completely different takes.

His mom mentioned a woman around Minsik's age who'd been in his Sunday school class. She'd recently divorced and was attending their church again. Emphasizing that the woman had no kids and had divorced after two years, just like Minsik, she suggested he come to church this week and say hi. Minsik flat-out refused, saying he wasn't going to church, and that he definitely wasn't meeting this woman. At that, his mom pursed her lips and emptied her glass.

"Do you know why I never drank until now?" she asked.

"Because you go to church."

"The first miracle Jesus performed was turning water into wine at a wedding feast. Drinking isn't the problem. It's the mistakes you make after you drink."

"So are you saying you make mistakes when you drink?"

"No, not me. I can hold my liquor. Before I got married, male colleagues tried so hard to get me drunk, but I never did. It's just that I couldn't stand the taste. Soju's too bitter, beer's too bland, and wine's too sweet . . . But this beer is really good. It's got a nice aroma and a slightly bitter, nutty flavor that I really like," Mrs. Yeom said, munching on some dried seaweed.

Minsik's eyes lit up. This was it—the perfect moment to make his pitch. With his knack for timing, he sensed it was the ideal opportunity to bring up the brewery business. She liked the beer, and though she said she could handle her liquor, she looked a bit tipsy. If he offered her another drink and laid out his plan, she might just warm up to selling the store and investing in a brewery.

But they were out of beer. Glancing at the empty cans, Minsik decided to head back to the store. He grabbed his phone and sat down next to his mom.

Minsik dashed to the store and headed straight for the cooler, grabbing four cans of the ale. He took them to the counter, but the night-shift worker—Dokgon or Dokgeon or whatever his name was—was nowhere in sight. Where had that wacko vanished to now? Really, the guy couldn't be more of a nuisance. Minsik got a plastic bag from the counter and bagged the beers himself. Just then, the man emerged from the storeroom, arms full of noodle bowls stacked up to his chin. Minsik turned around, making sure his annoyance was clear. The man set the bowls down on a table by the window and walked over. Minsik pulled out his phone. As the man came closer, eyeing him suspiciously, Minsik thrust his phone at him.

"There's your proof! Happy now?"

Minsik flashed the selfie he'd taken with his mom five minutes earlier. For a long time, the man stared at the photo of Minsik and his slightly tipsy mom—both making finger hearts, their faces close together—then finally gave a nod. With a victorious grin, Minsik turned to leave, then he suddenly stopped.

"How much of this did you sell today?"

"You're the first today . . . I was going to tell the boss . . . to stop stocking them."

"What are you talking about? You haven't even tried it! She says it's great and told me to get more."

"Business . . . isn't about selling . . . what I like . . . It's about selling what other people like."

"People do like it!"

"Sales . . . don't lie."

"Hmph. Just wait and see," Minsik scoffed. He shoved open the door and left.

When he got home, Minsik found his mom snoring softly at the dining table, her flushed face buried in her arms. He stood there for a moment, watching her—a small figure with more white than black in her hair. Then he picked her up and carried her to the bedroom. She felt light in his arms, but his heart felt heavy.

After settling his mom in bed, Minsik returned to the dining table and cracked open a beer. He gulped down the golden ale he dreamed of making and selling one day—the first drink he'd shared with his mom, the drink that could turn his life around. With each sip, he let go of the thoughts and regrets that weighed him down.

It had been a good night. He'd toasted with his mom, shared stories, and even taken some photos together. He hadn't felt that kind of warmth in a long time, and that was enough for now. The talk about selling the store and the investment could wait until tomorrow. Since his mom liked the beer, he still had a chance. Let Mrs. Oh and that Dok-something-or-other figure out how to support themselves. Mrs. Oh wouldn't put up much of a fuss if she was let go, but that dimwit? He was a different story, and Minsik needed to look into him. After all, he couldn't let anyone interfere with his potential business plans, especially not some guy spouting nonsense about the lack of demand. If that continued, convincing his mom would get harder. Minsik needed to act fast.

He decided to do some digging. His mom had laughed off his questions about how the man was hired, which only raised more red flags. Clearly, the guy was trouble and needed to go. The first step was to look into his past. If Minsik found anything shady and reported it, his mom would have no choice but to fire him. He'd reach out to Mr. Kwak, a private investigator he knew from his days in Yongsan, first thing in the morning.

As he finished his beer, Minsik kept thinking about the evening with his mom. It seemed like they could get along again. He pulled out his phone and set the photo he'd taken with her as his wallpaper. Their clumsy finger hearts looked almost sweet.

7

Expired but Perfectly Fine

"Working part time at the store would be better than this," Kwak muttered to himself as he followed his subject from the convenience store toward Seoul Station. The guy, lumbering along in a white parka, resembled a polar bear that had lost its way. Meanwhile, Kwak felt like an old Eskimo, wandering aimlessly in the Arctic. Despite tracking the subject for three days, there had been zero payoff so far. Tailing someone who constantly roamed these freezing streets made Kwak wish he was just a worker cooped up inside the warm store, even if it meant earning minimum wage.

Kwak kicked himself for taking the job from Kang and lowered his mask, feeling suffocated. He hated wearing the KF94 masks so much that he hadn't worn one even during yellow dust storms, but now, with the world going to hell, they were expected to wear these all the time. Kwak sighed, only to be hit with the smell of his own breath. Adjusting his scarf, he tried to strengthen his resolve and recalled Kang's promise. "Find out who he is. As soon as you dig up his dirty past, you'll get two million." Kang had told him to hurry, saying the guy had appeared out of nowhere and was getting in the way of selling the convenience store, blocking plans for a new business.

Kwak had asked for half the money up front but got turned down, eventually settling for a measly 200,000 won. Kang then went to an ATM, withdrew the money through a credit card advance, and handed it over, saying, "Make it quick. If I run out of patience, I might just skip the investigation and get some friends to push him out myself."

Though Kang talked a big game, Kwak figured he probably wouldn't follow through with his threats, especially since he had resorted to hiring him. Having observed Kang for a while, Kwak was used to playing along and then laughing at Kang behind his back. In fact, taking on this case hurt his pride somewhat, but he had accepted it anyway, since there had been a time when he had benefited from Kang's more successful schemes. After all, he needed to scrape together whatever he could for his golden years. It was only after turning sixty that he began preparing for retirement. Now, as an elderly man living alone, his future hung on the savings he had just recently started cobbling together.

The only information Kang had provided was that the subject worked nights at the convenience store and went by the name of Dokgo. Was it Dokgo after *dokgeo*, as in *single*? *Damn it.*

Kwak felt a surge of anger at being reminded of his own age and loneliness. Regardless, his job was to find out whether Dokgo was a first or last name. Trailing someone as sluggish as a bear should have been a piece of cake for him, with his thirty years of experience in this line of work. But the guy just kept walking. He'd leave the store, walk past Seoul Station to Manridong Pass, then through Aeogae and Chungjeongno, toward his room in Dongja-dong. Or he'd head to Huam-dong past Yongsan High School, through Haebangchon and Bogwang-dong, past Ichon-dong and Yongsan Station, back toward his room in Dongja-dong. In any case, he roamed these neighborhoods like the Energizer Bunny.

Especially now, with the dreadful epidemic forcing everyone to wear masks, Kwak struggled to breathe and grew exhausted from the long daily treks. So, for the past three days, he could only follow the subject for half a day before giving up and retreating to his studio apartment in Wonhyoro.

But now, he couldn't put things off any longer. He wasn't learning anything, and he needed answers. Fueling up with a big breakfast, Kwak was determined to follow his subject until the end of the day. He slowly tailed him, keeping a few people between them, walking with a stoop customary to the elderly. Though it was the fourth day, the subject seemed completely unaware he was being followed. Just when Kwak was beginning to despair that the day would yield nothing again, the man veered off his path and entered Seoul Station. Quickening his pace, Kwak managed to position himself near the bottom of the escalator the man had taken.

Once inside the station, Kwak's eyes darted around for the white parka, but the place was packed with people in thick coats. There had to be a reason for someone who liked to roam the streets to suddenly head indoors, so the subject couldn't have left already. He had to be here. Kwak searched the station, peeking into a fast-food joint, a convenience store, and even a restroom, but there was no sign of him. Wondering if the man might be buying a train ticket, Kwak headed toward the ticketing area.

Just then, a breaking news report about a COVID-19 cluster infection in Daegu blared from a television screen in the center of the station. Kwak froze. He'd assumed the epidemic would blow over soon, but hearing about the virus spreading uncontrollably and the shortage of masks made him wonder how many he had at home. He shuddered. As he was a diabetic and therefore more vulnerable to infection, the news of this virus being particularly deadly to the elderly and those with underlying conditions felt as urgent as—or more urgent than—his current assignment.

While absorbed in the news, Kwak spotted the subject sitting among a group of homeless people behind the TV. *Bingo!* He pulled out his outdated flip phone, pretending to make a call while secretly snapping a photo of the man, who was sitting on his white parka, chatting with the homeless. The phone silently captured the image, which would serve as evidence for Kang. Kwak felt encouraged. His hunch that the subject's reluctance to stray from Seoul Station hinted at a homeless background was likely correct.

Kwak edged closer behind the TV. He saw the group eating convenience store lunch boxes and chatting with the subject. Though the scene resembled a den of beggars, there was an oddly warm atmosphere about it. Then, the man stood up, put on his white parka, waved to the group, and began walking away, likely heading toward the Seoul Station Plaza. Kwak crouched low as he approached the group and sat among them. They glanced at him warily and returned to their meals. Recalling the intimidating demeanor he'd honed during his detective days, Kwak flashed a fake police badge.

"Don't make a fuss. Just answer my questions, got it?" he demanded, trying to ignore the smell of body odor through his mask. They stared at Kwak with frightened expressions but continued fiddling with their chopsticks.

"You know the guy in the white parka? Is he a friend?"

"Not exactly," one of them replied.

"Then who is he?"

"He's more like a colleague," another said.

"But he's not homeless, right? Was he homeless before?"

"I don't know. He just came by and bought us food," a third person chimed in.

"You don't know him, but he bought you food? Why?"

"He's a bad guy," the third one muttered.

"What? The guy who bought you lunch is a bad guy?"

"No . . . you're the bad guy," the second one said.

"You morons think I'm just messing around here?" Kwak barked, making them flinch.

"This lunch box is really good," the first one said, picking up the rice with his chopsticks.

Damn it. Talking with them was a waste of time. Kwak had to hurry. He stood up, accepting that the investigation had failed. Just as he was about to leave, he noticed the third one smirking as he opened a bottle—a bottle of soda, not soju. Then the other two followed suit, cracking open their bottles. He looked closer and realized it wasn't soda. They were all drinking corn silk tea. They raised their bottles in a toast and drank. What the hell was going on here? Leaving the bizarre scene behind, Kwak hurried after the subject.

He quickly crossed the station, taking the escalator to the plaza, and spotted the white parka disappearing into the underground passage. By the time Kwak reached the stairs, the subject had bought a ticket from the machine and was entering Subway Line 1. Kwak rushed to catch up.

The subject got on the Cheongnyangni-bound train and stood by the door, staring into the dark void outside the window. Kwak took a seat across from him, ready to follow him off the train at any moment. Aside from the distinctive musty smell of Line 1, it was comfortable, and the warmth made everyone drowsy. Most passengers sat quietly, their faces half-hidden behind masks, while those without masks kept their heads down, mouths shut. The train felt more like a hospital ward, prompting Kwak to sigh again, only for his stale breath to bounce back at him.

At City Hall Station, a man in his mid-fifties wearing a thick coat entered, talking on the phone without a mask. Boasting a ruddy face and a beer belly protruding from his open coat, he sat across from Kwak and continued his loud conversation.

"So, put five K in Namyangju and spread the rest into Hoengseong . . . No, listen carefully, I said five thousand in Namyangju, got it? And for Hoengseong, personally check each address I sent you yesterday . . . Exactly. They've got prime selections there . . . Uh-huh . . ."

The man barked into his phone, turning the subway car into his personal office. Kwak couldn't help but wonder what those "prime selections" in Hoengseong were. By the time the call ended, everyone in the car was glaring at the man's maskless face. But then he dialed another number, humming and releasing several snorts as he waited. When the person on the other end picked up, he started up again in his booming voice.

"Ah, Director Oh, how are you? . . . Yup, yup . . . So, are we hitting the greens this weekend or what? Lake Park? Come on, let's go to New Country instead. There's a reason I need to go to New Country . . . That's right . . . Why don't we do Lake Park in the spring . . . New Country this time, okay? . . . Sure, dinner's on me, and a little something extra too . . . hee-hee . . ."

The man talked nonstop. Growing increasingly annoyed, Kwak shifted his gaze to the subject, but was startled to see him staring down at the top of the talkative man's head.

The man laughed and hung up, about to make another call, but the subject suddenly plopped into the empty seat beside him. When the man turned, the subject met his gaze with narrowed eyes.

"So . . . where did you decide to go?" the subject asked calmly.

"What? What did you say?" the man asked, eyes wide with disbelief.

"Are you going to . . . Lake Park? Or is it . . . New Country?" the subject asked, miming a golf swing.

"What? Who the hell are you?" the man said, adding more force to his already loud voice. "Why are you eavesdropping on people's conversations? Are you nuts?"

"Because we can all hear you," the subject said sharply.

For a moment, the man stared blankly at him. Suddenly, not just Kwak but everyone on the train was listening to the exchange between the two men. The car fell silent as the subject's cheeks twitched, his glare fixed on the man.

"I didn't care . . . which golf course you were going to this weekend . . . but you were so loud I got curious . . . Personally I prefer Lake Park in the spring . . . Yes, definitely go there in the spring . . . And Hoengseong . . . you said to spread the rest there, right? Where exactly? . . . I heard the market's booming . . . after they put in a new road for the Pyeongchang Olympics. You said that earlier . . . didn't you?"

The subject's words came out in short bursts, like a student learning to speak a foreign language. The man's face reddened, his fists clenching as he searched for a response. The subject leaned in closer, his bulky frame invading more and more of the man's personal space. The latter looked around uncomfortably, seeking help. However, Kwak, along with everyone else in the car, seemed to be enjoying the scene. Realizing he had no allies, the man awkwardly clicked his tongue. Just then, an announcement for Jongno 3-ga Station came on.

"First time I take the subway in years and run into all kinds of crazies," the man muttered, standing up to head for the door.

The subject also got to his feet and stood next to him.

"W-what the hell?" the man blurted.

"I'm getting off too . . . Can you tell me more . . . about that property in Hoengseong? You've got me so curious . . . I don't think I can sleep tonight."

"Are you serious?"

"Yup . . . I'm getting off with you."

"Ah, screw it! Do whatever you want!"

"But why . . . aren't you wearing a mask? Is it because . . . of your bad breath?"

Laughter erupted from behind people's masks, filling the subway car. The man's face flushed crimson as he yanked a crumpled mask from his coat pocket and glanced around, as though he felt unjustly accused.

"What the fuck? Sorry for being loud, okay? Happy now?" he snapped, bolting out as soon as the doors slid open, with the subject close on his heels.

Kwak hurried to follow. Leaving the snickers behind, he stepped off the train, maintaining a slower pace. Ahead, the man whirled around, saw the subject still following him, and fled in horror. Served him right. Who did he think he was? Did he think his wealth and size gave him the right to take over public spaces? The moment someone more intimidating confronted him, he ran.

As the man went up the exit stairs, the subject stopped following and turned toward the transfer area, probably heading to Line 3. Kwak let him move ahead, mulling over what had just happened. The loud jerk had called the man crazy, but to Kwak, he seemed sharp—maybe even honorable, a rare trait these days. And though it could have all been a bluff, he appeared to know his stuff about golf courses and real estate. Kwak's instincts told him that despite the subject's current lifestyle—working night shifts and mingling with the homeless—he could have had a privileged past that allowed him to afford such hobbies. Plus, Line 3 went to Gangnam . . . Seeing where he got off might peel back another layer of his identity. Nervously, Kwak waited on the platform for the Ogeum-bound train, keeping a discreet distance.

The subject exited at Apgujeong Station. Kwak watched him walk toward Hyundai High School. The wind was freezing, and Kwak clutched his scarf against its bite. *If I catch a cold and get really sick, what will happen to me?* Suddenly, the subject stopped and stared up at a building, deep in thought. Then he turned and glanced in Kwak's direction. Kwak quickly ducked, pretending to tie his shoe, stealing a glance only to see the subject's white parka disappearing into the building.

Kwak rushed over and stood in front of the building. The chic, five-story structure, all done up in exposed brick, was a hospital—specifically a plastic surgery clinic. Excitement surged within him as his detective instincts kicked in. Digging into this clinic could reveal something about the subject's past or what he was up to, since he clearly hadn't come for a procedure. At the very least, the subject had either worked here or was looking for someone who did. Now Kwak had one task. Settling into a window seat at a coffee shop next door, he began his stakeout.

Before he could even finish his cup of coffee, though, the subject stepped back out of the building. So much for a stakeout. Wearing a blank expression, the man headed back toward the subway station, and after a moment's thought, Kwak drained the rest of his coffee and stood up. That was enough shadowing for one day. He headed toward the clinic where the subject had spent about twenty minutes.

As a young man, Kwak had often driven without a license. He'd even known a guy who'd carried a fake license. The logic was simple: If you were a good driver, chances were you wouldn't crash. And if you didn't crash, you wouldn't get caught. In other words, having the skills and looking the part were nearly as good as having legitimate credentials. Kwak used his fake police ID in much the same way. Though he'd had to leave the force over an unfortunate incident, he still saw himself as a cop at heart. For someone like him, duping a clinic receptionist wouldn't be difficult.

The sight of the immaculate, upscale lobby made him a little anxious, but Kwak flashed his police ID at the reception desk and said he needed details about the man who had just left, claiming he was a witness in a case. The receptionist, however, kept repeating she didn't know anything, her smooth, unlined face betraying no emotion. Confronted with this surprisingly rigid woman, Kwak threatened to return with a warrant. She frowned and said the man had met with the director and that she knew nothing more. Kwak was wondering whether he needed to meet the director when a man in his early fifties, wearing his coat, emerged and scrutinized him. Immediately, the receptionist informed him that a police officer had arrived, pointing at Kwak. The tall, large-headed director approached, his right cheekbone twitching. His face was flushed and puffy, with faint swelling along his jawline. After giving Kwak an unpleasant once-over, he curtly instructed Kwak to follow him and turned on his heels, heading into his office. *All right, let's get to the bottom of this*, Kwak thought as he followed.

Sitting in front of the coffee table in the pristine, stylish office, Kwak felt his tension rise. The director made him wait until a receptionist brought drinks, and finally sat across from him, sizing him up.

"Which unit did you say you were with?"

"I'm with the Yongsan Intelligence Crime Team."

Kwak flashed his ID, but the director didn't bother glancing at it and made a phone call instead. Kwak gulped. The director started speaking to someone on the other end, and then asked Kwak for his name again. *Wait, this isn't how it's supposed to go . . .* Left without a choice, he stated the pseudonym on his ID again and felt cold sweat break out on his forehead. Staring at Kwak with narrowed eyes, the director repeated Kwak's fake name to the person on the phone. Soon after, he put down the phone and smiled at Kwak.

"They say there's no one by that name in the Yongsan Intelligence Crime Team."

"That can't be right. Let me—"

"Aren't you the one committing a crime here?"

The director leaned back, eyeing Kwak with a casual, amused look. The tables had turned. Kwak had met a formidable opponent and knew he was about to be humiliated. As the director gave him a look that said "Let's see you crawl out of this," Kwak discarded whatever dignity he had left and decided to exploit his age.

"Look, I used to be a cop. I had to lie because this is an urgent matter. I hope you can understand."

"I don't know how urgent this is, but I caught you in the act. Care to explain?"

"The man you just met—he's my nephew. Been looking for him and finally tracked him down, but he won't tell me what's going on, so I took matters into my own hands and ended up here."

The director nodded slightly, weighing Kwak's words as if equipped with a lie detector. Then he smacked his lips and glared at Kwak.

"Patients who come here often change their stories, so everything in this room is recorded. That means we've got you on tape impersonating a police officer. How about you drop the act and tell the truth? This is your last chance."

The director's tone had shifted, becoming sharp and condescending. He was a nasty, tenacious SOB. Realizing that quick surrender was the only option, Kwak admitted he ran a detective agency and was investigating the man on behalf of a client. He bowed in apology, stooping low enough to reveal his bald crown.

He wasn't sure at which point his confession was accepted, but the director's expression softened. Then, as if he were a judge dealing with a remorseful defendant, he said, "So, detective agencies still exist. What have you learned so far?"

"Not much . . . just that he's been mingling with homeless people at Seoul Station and that he came here. That's all."

"I guess you're not too good at your job. I have no use for you, but I'll cut you some slack if you can prove otherwise."

Kwak knew the director was squeezing him for information, yet he found himself cooperating.

"Oh, he works at a convenience store! Covers nights at a store in Cheongpa-dong and drifts around Seoul Station and Yongsan during the day. To be honest, he doesn't seem to be all there."

"He's moonlighting at a convenience store?"

The director started laughing. This man, so reserved until now, was letting his guard down. Maybe, Kwak thought, he could manage to crawl out of this humiliation, and everything would turn out okay. But then, the director stopped laughing and fixed him with a cold stare.

"A convenience store . . . that's funny, but inconvenient for me. Tell me, does your little operation handle cleanups?"

"What do you mean by 'cleanups'?"

"Never mind. Just find out where he lives, where he goes when he's usually alone. Get me that information, and you'll be compensated."

"If you don't mind me asking, what kind of compensation are we talking about?" Kwak ventured cautiously.

"Let's just say I won't press charges."

"Th-thank you."

The director abruptly demanded to see Kwak's phone. Kwak handed over his old phone and watched as the director flipped it open and dialed a number. Soon after, something vibrated from inside a desk drawer, and the director pulled out what looked like a burner phone.

"Call me in three days. Don't disappear. While I'm at it, I might decide to take care of you too."

Kwak nodded, his lips trembling. He stood up, bowed, and turned to leave. He wanted to escape as quickly as possible. He shuddered at his own foolishness, for not having realized the danger he was in.

Just as he reached the door, a sharp "Wait" from the director stopped him. Kwak composed his expression and turned around.

"Who asked you to get info on that bastard?"

"Disclosing client details is a breach of confidentiality . . . I'm sorry," Kwak replied, clinging to the last vestiges of professional integrity. The director burst into laughter again, looking at Kwak with scorn.

"Whoever it is, if they want him gone, consider it done. Tell them there's no need to worry. As for you, you can sit back and enjoy the show. And when he disappears, say you did it and collect your fee."

Kwak left the clinic and walked aimlessly until he found himself beneath the Dongho Bridge. He climbed the stairs and walked across, the biting wind lashing against his face as the river stretched endlessly from south to north. He paused, gazing down at the dark blue waters moving slowly, unstoppable as the flow of time. Suddenly, he felt the urge to join that flow. Should he jump? Nothing in the world would change if he disappeared. The humiliation he'd experienced at the clinic seemed like a preview of his feeble, worthless future. It was unbearable.

Kwak pulled his fake police ID from his wallet. The photo, from when he was in his forties and still on the force, now seemed like a ridiculous joke, a pathetic lie. He hurled the ID into the Han River instead of himself.

After crossing to the north side, Kwak warmed himself in a large bookstore in Jongno before heading to meet his old friend Hwang. At a BBQ restaurant near Nakwon Arcade, Kwak drank soju in silence. Hwang, who worked alternate days as a security guard for an apartment complex, told Kwak to quit the detective business and consider security work. Though Hwang admitted he felt lousy when dealing with the general public, he said there wasn't much else for men their age.

Kwak was almost convinced.

However, after three bottles of soju, Hwang's bitter venting spoiled even the flavor of the meat. "Damn it. I have to head back soon . . . Got to sleep and wake up at the crack of dawn," Hwang said. "My hangovers last too long these days . . . Shit . . . I need to hit the sack early . . . This on-off schedule isn't for old men . . ."

"Why don't you take it easy for a bit?"

"I need to bring home at least one and a half million won . . . If I don't, my wife won't even cook for me. Back when I was younger and raking it in, she couldn't do enough . . . but now, I'm less than the dog to her. Maybe I should have just gotten a divorce in my twilight years like you."

"You think I'm happy, living alone?"

"We shouldn't be treated this way just because we're old. We helped build this country, we raised families . . . so why? The kids hardly ever call, and the world looks at us like we're garbage."

"Come on now."

"Do you know what security guards have to do? Part of my job is separating trash. The smell of food waste could knock you over . . . and then I'm the one who has to rinse out those bins. It's disgusting. And that's not all. You know the difference between recyclables and trash? No, right? Well, some folks dump trash in the recycling bin, saying it's recyclables. When I tell them it's not and to slap a waste sticker on it, they look at me like *I'm* the trash. Makes me want to toss them in the bin myself, fuck."

As Hwang's drunken tirade grew louder, Kwak felt the stares from nearby tables. His griping seemed only to prove he was indeed disposable. Kwak poured him another shot, as if trying to grease a squeaky wheel. Hwang emptied his glass and continued ranting about his family and society. Why did he have to be so loud?

Kwak couldn't take it anymore. He placed his hand firmly on Hwang's shoulder, silencing him. Hwang looked up, confused.

"You said your family can't stand you, right?"

"Yup . . . They think I'm a loser."

"That's tough. But honestly, if I were them, I'd probably feel the same. Who wants to be around someone who just complains all the time?"

"What? I can't talk about my feelings?"

Kwak sighed wearily at Hwang's indignance. "What are you even complaining about? What do you know? Did you study as much as the kids these days? Or read a bunch of books?"

"I've experienced a lot. What's so great about all that studying? Whose side are you on?"

"Me? I'm on the side of whoever keeps quiet. Listen, old folks like us, without money or influence, don't get a say. You know why success is great? It gives you a voice. Look at the old people who've made it. Even past seventy, they still call the shots in politics and business. When they speak, the younger ones listen. Even their kids respect them. But us? We're finished. So what's left to complain about?"

"Shit, you're right. We're washed-up losers . . . Then why don't we losers get together and say whatever we want? How about we hit Gwanghwamun this weekend and make some noise? Come on, man, being divorced isn't the end of the world! Let's go scream our lungs out at Gwanghwamun this weekend, okay?"

Kwak felt a wave of embarrassment, for both Hwang and himself. He stood up, snatched Hwang's mask off the table, and slapped it over Hwang's gaping mouth. Enough was enough. He wanted Hwang to shut up, to stay away from the Gwanghwamun Square rallies where old folks tended to gather, and to avoid catching COVID.

He paid the bill, and as he walked out, he could still hear Hwang's angry muttering behind him. Another friend was crossed off his dwindling list.

Was it the depressing drinks with Hwang or the humiliation at the clinic earlier? Kwak couldn't bring himself to go home. After all, home was just a cold, dark studio apartment with no light, no warmth, no conversation—practically a prelude to a coffin. But in this weather, there was nowhere else to go. As Kwak walked the cold streets, he wondered where his life had gone wrong.

When his daughter decided to play sports in school and his son wanted to attend an arts high school, Kwak suddenly needed a considerable sum of money. The bribe that landed in his lap seemed like the perfect solution. He took the cash, disguised as a reward, and used it to buy his son's instrument and cover his lesson fees. But the price was steeper than he'd imagined. That bribe, which he'd accepted for the sake of his family, ended up costing him his career and his honor.

When he started running a detective agency, skirting the line between what was legal and illegal, he sensed his wife and kids pulling away. Damn it, who actually wanted to do this kind of work? He only did it because he needed to make money. Though the work was difficult, rough, and humiliating, he managed to make a living and even put his kids through college.

But now, his skills had deteriorated. He couldn't keep up with real private investigators. When he stopped bringing in money, his authority as the head of the family crumbled. Eventually, his wife had enough and asked for a divorce. The kids moved out the minute they hit adulthood, only calling occasionally when they remembered they had a dad.

He couldn't blame them, really. Although he hadn't been able to see it at the time, he acknowledged his role in it all. Living alone for the past two years had given him plenty of opportunity to look back and reflect. Kwak came to realize he didn't know how to do anything. His cooking was limited to instant noodles, and he couldn't even operate a washing machine. Conversations with his kids were awkward and strained, and it was the same with his ex-wife. He'd never resorted to violence, but he'd often yelled and lost his temper. His children had grown up witnessing this kind of behavior. Ultimately, he was responsible for his own solitude.

Now, without a family to talk to and knowing he only had himself to blame, the mask covering his mouth didn't seem so bad. Maybe he should have clamped his mouth shut with it a long time ago. Each time a harsh word he'd hurled at his family echoed in his head, the phrase "you reap what you sow" hit home harder.

Sobered by the late winter chill, he passed city hall and Namdaemun, reaching Seoul Station, where he saw a few homeless people. His steps automatically turned toward Cheongpa-dong. He needed to catch a bus back to Wonhyoro, but he felt compelled to return to the place where his journey had begun that day, to finally speak to the silent, bearlike figure he'd been following. He wanted to drop the act, to use whatever right he still had to speak, and to get the answers he needed. Kwak wanted to tell the man how he'd spent the past few days trailing him, to ask if he roamed the streets for similar reasons as Kwak, and to find out who he really was.

Kwak hesitated when he arrived at the convenience store. Inside, the subject was chatting with an elderly woman at the counter. She didn't seem to be a customer, judging by the fact that there weren't any purchases on the counter. When she gestured toward a shelf and the subject got out from behind the counter to rearrange some items, Kwak figured she was the store owner. The realization that she was Kang's mother made him stop in his tracks.

As he was debating whether to leave, the elderly woman opened the door and stepped out, waving at the subject with a smile before going on her way. She seemed not much older than Kwak, but if she was Kang's mother, she had to be in her seventies at least. Thinking that this kind-looking elder must have her own struggles because of her troublesome son, Kwak pushed open the door and stepped inside.

"Hello!"

Avoiding eye contact with the subject, who greeted him a beat late, Kwak headed straight for the cooler. Why was he so thirsty in winter? Maybe his mind was too preoccupied. Wanting to clear his head and quench his thirst, he grabbed four 500-milliliter beers and went to the counter.

"If you take this out . . . and add one of these . . . it'll be ten thousand won for the four cans."

"Really?"

"Yes. Right now, it's thirteen thousand seven hundred won . . . but if you switch this one . . . for that one, it'll save you three thousand seven hundred won."

"Uh . . . I see."

Kwak swapped out a beer for another as suggested and declined the offer of a plastic bag. After paying, he put two cans in his parka pockets and carried the remaining two in his hands, heading for the empty table outside. Feeling the chill from the green can, he cracked one open and took a sip. He felt instantly refreshed, and an unexpected burp escaped him.

Just then, the store door opened, and the subject stepped out, setting something next to Kwak and turning it on. It was a heater. The warmth spread quickly, making Kwak feel as though someone were sitting next to him. Kwak nodded in thanks toward the subject, who had already retreated inside.

The man's kindness caught Kwak off guard. He had treated Kwak as he would any other customer, saving him money and showing consideration. This unexpected hospitality dissolved any intentions Kwak had of confronting him. Kwak savored his winter beer. After two cans, the heat from the heater wasn't just warming his body but his insides as well.

Just then, the door jingled again, and the subject reappeared. He sat down across from Kwak, with what looked like a hot dog in each hand, and offered one to Kwak.

"Sir, this here . . . is called a hot bar . . . it's really good . . . I just heated them up in the microwave . . . How about we each have one?"

Kwak tried to act nonchalant as he eyed the so-called hot bar. Steam rose from the sausages, making his mouth water. Still, he couldn't help feeling suspicious, wondering if the subject knew who he was and was testing him.

"Why are you giving this to me?"

"It's not good to drink . . . on an empty stomach. On a cold night like this . . . a hot bar will warm you up. Plus, these . . . just expired. We can't sell them anyway . . . but they're perfectly fine to eat. So don't worry about it."

Speaking in spurts, the subject stretched out his hand once more. Kwak's expression softened at the explanation. He accepted the sausage and took a bite. The hot, juicy meat tasted good. He chewed silently, glancing at his companion, who also seemed to be enjoying his food.

"Is it good?" the subject asked, his mouth full.

Good? Kwak nodded and bit into the hot bar again, as if he hadn't eaten for days. He cracked open a new beer and took a swig, only to be overwhelmed by tears. The sudden emotional outburst shook him, and soon he was sobbing, his shoulders quaking. The subject came around the table and placed a hand on Kwak's shoulder, this time clearly asking if he was okay. Kwak wiped his tears with his sleeve and looked up.

"I'm fine, but you need to be careful. Someone's after you," Kwak said cautiously.

The subject cocked his head, confused.

"You went to the plastic surgery clinic in Apgujeong today, didn't you?" Kwak asked.

At that, the subject's expression changed, his pupils dilating beneath his small eyes. He fixed a stare on Kwak, asking how he knew. The sudden shift was chilling, and Kwak felt as if he were being interrogated by a fierce prosecutor from his police days. Kwak disclosed everything: how he had tailed the subject for four days at the request of the convenience store owner's son, the subject's interactions with the homeless at Seoul Station, his visit to the plastic surgery clinic, and the clinic director's intentions to get rid of him.

"He even asked me where you live. I know where your room is, but I didn't tell him that. I don't know what's between you two, but it's clear he wants you gone."

After listening quietly to Kwak's story, the subject's cheeks began to twitch. The twitching soon turned into laughter, a hearty laugh that made Kwak feel as though he were being mocked. The man abruptly stopped and stared at Kwak, serious once more.

"Sir. Thank you . . . but you don't need to worry."

The subject smiled and went back to chewing his hot bar, seemingly unbothered. With nothing left to say, Kwak felt empty. He finished his remaining beer.

Finally, the man spoke again. "But why did the owner's son . . . ask you to investigate me?"

"Well, he said ever since you started working here, sales have gone up, and now he can't sell the store. The store needs to be struggling for his mom to consider selling."

"Hmm."

"What is it?"

"Look around. You've been here half an hour . . . and not one customer has come in . . . Business isn't good, but the owner won't sell . . . I guarantee it. Whether I go or stay won't make a difference."

"Why's that?"

"She isn't running this place to make a profit . . . She can live comfortably on her teacher's pension . . . She keeps it running . . . just to give us jobs."

"But with her son so fixated on the money, she'll eventually . . ." Kwak trailed off, leaving the sentence unfinished. Kwak had witnessed quiet confidence in Kang's mother's dignified demeanor, and now he saw the same resolve in the subject. Having spent over forty years dealing with lies as both a cop and a detective, he recognized genuine conviction when he saw it.

"Tell your client . . . his mom will never sell the store . . . Oh, I guess you'll get paid if you figure me out . . . and get rid of me? Just say you did it . . . and collect your fee."

"What do you mean?"

"I'm . . . quitting."

With a smile, the subject pointed toward the entrance. A HELP WANTED sign was stuck to the glass door. *Well, I'll be damned.*

He had always prided himself on his observational skills, but he'd missed an obvious clue right under his nose. Kwak realized it was time for him to retire.

He got up and went over to read the ad. It was for the night shift, from 10:00 p.m. to 8:00 a.m., offering an hourly wage of nine thousand won, just above minimum wage. *Night shifts*, he mused. *Not too bad.*

He settled back down across from the subject, who was calmly sipping something. It was corn silk tea. Noticing Kwak's surprise, he wiped his mouth and explained, "Ah, I quit drinking . . . this is actually pretty good."

"But where will you go if you quit? From what I've seen these past few days, you don't have many places to go besides your room and here."

"Sir, you've got my routine . . . all figured out."

"What's there to figure out? Thanks to you, I've done way more than my share of walking in this cold."

"You're right. I've been walking a lot lately . . . It helps when you've got so much on your mind. I've decided to leave Seoul . . . It's been a long time coming, but I finally worked up the courage . . . I just need to find someone to take over here . . . then I'm off. Does that answer your question?"

Kwak nodded and gave a small smile. The situation was peculiar. He was having a conversation with the very person he was hired to track, and this person had just given him a tip on how to wrap up the investigation. Kwak was surprised to find himself genuinely concerned for the subject's future and relieved that he had a plan. Most of all, he liked the warmth of this place—the heat tickling his sides, the large man opposite him blocking the wind, and the owner's determination to keep the store open for her employees' sake.

"So . . . are you a detective or something?" the subject asked, his eyes full of curiosity.

"Well, you could say that. Just call me P.I. Kwak."

"In that case . . . would you accept a job from me? I'm looking for a P.I."

What was this now—a *second* unexpected job offer? It was just what Kwak needed to further complicate his day. Noticing Kwak's hesitation, the subject added with a hopeful look, "Of course, I'll pay. How much do you charge?"

"I'll give you a discount. But who are you looking for? If you give me a name and their ID number, I can find them easily."

"Yes. I understand," the subject said.

Kwak nodded, agreeing to take on the assignment.

"But . . . if the person has passed away, can you still find them?"

"Absolutely."

The subject smiled brightly and nodded.

After taking a moment to catch his breath, Kwak asked, "So about this night shift—could an old man like me apply?"

"Definitely," the subject said, leaning forward, his eyes lit up with eagerness.

"And what about a guy like me, rough around the edges with no customer experience—think I could handle this job?"

"Sir, didn't you say you work in a detective agency? That's basically . . . a high-intensity service job, isn't it? Dealing with all sorts of difficult, shady people . . . Here, aside from one PIA granny who wants a refund on her half-eaten ice cream because it's too cold for her teeth, all our customers are gentle lambs."

"A PIA granny?"

"PIA . . . stands for pain in the ass. Anyway . . . you'd do just fine."

Eager to find his replacement and make his exit, the subject assured Kwak he could easily handle the job, even mentioning some YouTube videos to help him get started.

Kwak was convinced. After finishing his beer, he looked earnestly at the subject. "Once I wrap up your case, I'm switching careers. Can you tell the owner I'm interested in the position?"

"I'll let her know . . . Just get your CV and cover letter ready. And please . . . make it quick."

Kwak nodded, then popped open another beer, while the subject took another sip of his corn silk tea. They toasted to their new beginning just as three young men entered the store. The subject acknowledged them with a nod, put on his mask, and returned to his duties inside.

Kwak finished his beer, and before putting his mask back on, drank in the crisp winter air.

8

Always Convenience

What happens when you're lost in a single thought, twenty-four hours a day, seven days a week? And what if that thought is wrapped in excruciating memories? The more your brain soaks in the pain, the heavier it gets, and then you fall into the endless sea of sadness, and this brain turns into a massive anchor, dragging you down into the abyss. Soon, you're breathing differently—not through your nose, mouth, or gills—yet you insist you're still human, though you're living as something less. You try to forget, drowning your brain with alcohol, even ignoring hunger, but most of your memories evaporate, leaving you unable to say who you even are.

Around that time, I met an old homeless man. I used the last of my strength to get to Seoul Station, but I couldn't bring myself to step outside and sank to the ground, trembling with fear. That's when he took me under his wing. When he asked my name, I couldn't answer. I was tormented by headaches every time I tried to remember. I knew nothing beyond moving between trash cans and the food service in front of the station, but he led me to free meal services in Jongno and a hideout in the Euljiro underground passage. He taught me the ins and outs of the homeless shelters.

Without him, I would have died. My body, unlike my mind, seemed to remember my past, and many health issues came flooding in. If he hadn't arranged for me to receive urgent care and medication at a volunteer clinic, I wouldn't be here now. Of course, mixing the meds with soju didn't exactly help, but it at least slowed my march toward death.

We drank a lot together. He was more hooked than I was, always drunk, as if being intoxicated was the only way he could protect himself. Though he said we should never beg, when we ran out of booze, he somehow found the money for more soju and, precious as it was, never hesitated to share it with me. He was often harassed by the homeless clan at Seoul Station, so maybe he needed someone big to watch his back. Or maybe a secretary. Rumor had it he used to be an executive at a major corporation that went under during the IMF crisis.

He spent his days talking to me, killing time. We'd watch TV at the station, discussing politics, sports—whatever was on the news. After a year of this, I learned a lot. It was a different kind of education than what I'd known, more about the stories and emotions of people living on the fringes. Soon I experienced them firsthand. The only thing we never shared was our past. It stayed sealed between us, an unspoken rule, unknown and inexpressible.

Then one day, after I'd been at Seoul Station for about two years, my friend died, curled up beside me. There was nothing I could do. Should I have given him mouth-to-mouth? Or called an ambulance? As dawn broke and he slipped away, all I could do was sit next to him, sharing my body heat, repeating to myself the last thing he'd said the night before. His final words.

Dokgo. He told me his name was Dokgo and asked me to keep

his memory alive. Damn it. He didn't have the strength to clarify if Dokgo was his first or last name, and I didn't have the heart to ask. The next morning, he was gone. And to remember him, I became Dokgo.

For the next two years, I didn't leave Seoul Station. Didn't bother going to Jongno, Euljiro, or any shelters. Once I figured out how to take care of all my needs at the station, I truly felt homeless. As if trying to live up to the name Dokgo, I roamed solo, using loneliness as my shield. I could handle two guys on my own, but if three or more jumped me, I'd end up taking a beating and have to go to a clinic. Sometimes my heart would race, I couldn't pee, or my face would puff up like a steamed bun, but seeing it as part of dying, it didn't seem too bad.

At first, I tried digging up my past, but that quickly seemed pointless. Spending my days alone, I forgot how to talk properly, developed a stutter. But that was fine. It made people more sympathetic, helped me scrape together booze money. I got good at croaking out in a trembling voice, "I'm hungry . . . I'm really . . . hungry . . ."

That day, I was after a couple of punks from the gang on the first floor of the station. They'd swiped my booze a few days back, and I was ready to give them a beating. If I didn't, they'd rip me off again. Around there, you had to watch your back, even if you had nothing to steal. But just when I came up behind them, they took off, giddy, one of them clutching a little pink bag. *Ah, two birds with one stone,* I thought, and chased down those bastard thieves.

I roughed them up and grabbed the bag. I hunkered down in my hideout and opened the bag, feeling smug. But it had more than just a wallet and a coin purse. There was a bankbook, an ID, a notebook, and an OTP token—a whole load of important stuff. It hit me that if things went sideways, I could end up in deep with the cops. My head started pounding, so I just crashed, using the little bag as my pillow. I was hungry, but sleep had become more important than food for a while now.

I couldn't sleep long. The face of the bag's owner kept haunting me. Judging by the ID photo and her age, she was an elderly lady, and her kind face made me toss and turn. I opened the bag again and flipped through the notebook. On the last page, her personal info and phone number were neatly written, with the note: "If found, please call this number. You will be compensated." That "please" made me feel human, if only for a moment, and I found myself getting to my feet. I went to a pay phone and called her using the coins from her coin purse. Soon, a worried voice filled my ear. She said she'd come back to Seoul Station.

That's how I first met the boss.

This is Always Convenience, a small store on a Cheongpa-dong side street. I've spent many nights here now, but how I got here still feels like a dream. The perks? Escaping the cold winter nights and no more hunger pangs. The downside? I had to quit drinking, but somehow, I've managed so far. Taking her offer must have triggered my last bit of survival instinct. Like a pregnant stray seeking shelter to give birth, I must have been seeking a haven, even willing to give up booze, because there was something I still needed to do.

Once I stopped drinking, started eating properly, and found a warm place to crash, my health improved. Being able to relax and sleep in my little room during the day made me feel like I'd checked into some rehab. I woke up refreshed for the night shift, as if my illnesses had vanished. Although I'd always leaned more toward death than life, I now felt myself slowly rising, finding balance. Amazingly, my brain started to wake up too. Answering my coworkers' questions made my thinking sharper, and even my stutter started to improve with each customer interaction.

I was becoming human again, my frozen brain finally thawing. The ice wall between my memories and reality began to melt, revealing chunks of my past like pieces of a glacier. My memories rose like zombies, clawing at me. Even as they came for me, I tried to recognize their faces, finding a way to endure.

As I got used to the job, my memories started coming back. One early morning, a woman and her young daughter walked in, and the atmosphere changed instantly. They moved through the aisles like they were in an art gallery, chatting with affection. Hearing the mother ask her daughter what she liked, and the girl respond in her clear voice, filled me with a warmth that stirred something deep inside. When they finally brought their choices to the counter, I couldn't bring myself to look up, scared that meeting their eyes would cause my legs to buckle.

It was only after they paid and turned to leave that I dared to look. Watching them go, I suddenly remembered—I had a wife and a daughter. Did I call out her name then? My daughter's name? They both turned at the sound, but when I saw their faces, I was too terrified to keep walking down the path where my memories were taking me.

I started sinking again. During the night, I stood watch at the store, and during the day, I hid away in the curtained darkness of my room, which felt like a coffin. With my hunger gone, the old urge to drink started creeping back, but I fought it off with corn silk tea. Why corn silk tea? Well, when I was looking for something nonalcoholic, it was on a buy-one-get-one deal. Whether it was the placebo effect or not, the tea seemed to quench my thirst and took the edge off my craving for alcohol, even just a little.

A month into the job, after deducting the 1 million won advance from the boss, I managed to stash away about 800,000 won. The monthly wage from working nights at the store was more than what I'd scraped together from begging and scavenging over the last few years. With no place to spend it, I just folded the bills and stuffed them into my parka pocket, then pretty much forgot about it. The boss kept telling me to get my canceled ID sorted out, open a bank account, and get a card, but I'd been dragging my feet, not feeling up to it. When I first landed here, I wound up at the police station after defending the boss from some delinquents at the store. That's when I found out my real name and social security number. No criminal record, luckily. I left the police station and ditched my real name right away.

Because the moment I get a new ID, I'd have to start living for real. And if I started living for real, the pain would come back. I didn't have the guts to confront my past and all the dim memories that would come with it. What was the point of waking up all that trauma that led me to cut ties with the past in the first place?

I kept thinking about just making it through the winter. Maybe it was fear, haunted by the winter when old man Dokgo passed away. Maybe the memory of his cold, stiff back had driven me to seek a warmer place. And what's warmer than a convenience store? I resolved to spend this winter as comfortably as possible, to muster whatever strength I had left. Come spring, I planned to shed even the name Dokgo and become truly nameless, soaring into the sky. While I still had the strength, I was going to leave Seoul Station and leap from the bridge over the big river that cuts through this city. This winter, I vowed to gather the courage to make that jump.

But the image of my wife didn't fade. My conviction that I had a wife and daughter somewhere became clearer over time. Now I can remember every detail of my wife's face and gestures. She was short, with bobbed hair, so quiet she was almost silent. She was a woman of few words, always thoughtful, meeting my crankiness and ego with a smile. Until one day. I recall the day she got angry. What made her look at me with such loathing? Even as she glared at me, she didn't say much, which only made me angrier. The memory of her pushing my hands away and packing her bags came rushing back.

Jolted back to reality by the door chime, I realized I'd been dozing off at the counter. While an early-morning customer picked up items to start their day, I gulped down the corn silk tea next to me. I had to sip the amber liquid again and again to stop those fragments of memory, the ones I had drowned in booze, from rising back to the surface.

Seonsuk still looked at me like I was some kind of animal. If the streets taught me anything, it's how to read people's stares in a second. Most of the glances I got during my time at Seoul Station were pity mixed with disgust, maybe 30 percent to 70 percent. Some were genuinely concerned, and believe it or not, some even envied me, though they didn't know it.

But Seonsuk's gaze was different—10 percent pity, 90 percent disgust. It didn't bother me. She was the one who felt awkward, the one who got tired when it was time for the shift change. She'd always urge me to go home right after my shift, even when I tidied up outside and wiped down the table. I was doing a good thing, but she didn't like seeing me linger. Still, I did what I thought was right, because I wanted to repay the boss for giving me the chance to spend my last winter in peace.

There was an old, white-haired lady from the neighborhood who saw some good in me. She had to be past eighty, shuffling around stooped over with her snakelike scarf. One day, as I was wiping down the outdoor table, she asked me why I bothered cleaning it every day in the middle of winter when no one would use it. I told her I was wiping off pigeon poop. She seemed pleased—guess she wasn't a fan of pigeons or their droppings.

The next day, she came by with a group of grannies from the neighborhood, like they were on a little outing. They liked the store's specials and started bringing their grandkids along to take advantage of the buy-two-get-one deals. Once, to thank the white-haired lady for helping boost sales, I carried a set of drinks she'd bought right to her door. She must have spread the word at the senior center, because soon after, other ladies started asking me to haul their stuff home too. Some even gave me their addresses and asked if I could drop off their purchases later. I had no reason to say no—I had nothing else to do, and tiring myself out meant I'd sleep better back in my small room. Plus, when I delivered their bags, those ladies would hand me some rice cakes, sugar twists, or fruit to thank me.

They became like grandmothers, mothers, and aunts to me. Through them, I felt a bit of the maternal warmth I barely remembered. I could feel it slowly warming me from the inside. The only tricky part was enduring their endless questions: "Married yet?" "Divorced already?" "Want me to find you a nice girl?" "How old are you?" "Interested in meeting my niece?" "What kind of work did you do before this?" "You go to church?" "How'd you like to work at our family orchard?" They bounced between general and personal questions, their dentures clicking as they spoke. I had no choice but to cycle through "No," "I don't have one," "I'm fine, thank you," and "That's all right." After a few rounds of this, they figured I'd had a rough life and stopped prodding. Except for the white-haired lady. She'd ask every time she saw me, like it was a tune she couldn't stop humming: "What did you do before? I'm too old to be of much help, but I've got to know. I just can't stand not knowing. What brought a fine young man like you here?"

Ma'am, I'm not quite sure myself, but when I figure it out, I'll let you know. After all, you've been so kind to me, and I want to satisfy your curiosity.

Looking back, maybe her relentless questions kept me asking myself who I really was.

Meanwhile, Seonsuk wasn't thrilled with the busier mornings, often muttering about the small bump in business from a few old folks. But with sales rising and the boss pleased, she bit her tongue. She knew that if sales dropped too much and the store closed, she'd be out of a job.

Near the end of the year, Seonsuk suddenly apologized. She said she was sorry for any misunderstanding and suggested we try to get along better in the new year. I told her the fried chicken from our store was the best, especially the batches she made. She laughed, then started venting, telling me I understood her better than the men in her life. She sighed and said talking to her son was like talking to a brick wall. Seeing her so dejected hit me hard, and the phrase "like talking to a brick wall" stunned me. Was it my wife or my daughter who'd said that to me before leaving? With that look of profound disappointment, as if there were no point in talking anymore? Could it have been both? I just couldn't figure it out.

Around this time, Sihyeon, who'd trained me, got scouted by another convenience store. I didn't know convenience store workers could get scouted, and I was even more surprised when she handed me an electric razor, saying it was thanks to me. I ran my fingers over the scruffy stubble on my chin, holding the gift. She told me to take care of myself, and I wished her luck.

With Sihyeon gone, the workload for Seonsuk and me got heavier. At the start of the new year, as soon as Seonsuk came to work, she burst into tears. I hurried over to try to comfort her, but what could I do? I handed her some corn silk tea. Drinking the tea seemed to calm her down. She took a couple of deep breaths, then started talking about her son. It sounded like their relationship had fallen apart, and her son was burned out from his derailed life. But getting back on track wasn't easy, and this world wasn't the kind of place where staying on track guaranteed you'd end up somewhere good. I didn't have much to say, so I just listened. I wondered how desperate she must have been to spill all this to me.

To put yourself in someone else's shoes. That phrase only started to make sense to me after my life veered off course. Up until that point, it had been a one-way street. Everyone listened to me, my feelings always came first, and those who disagreed with me were shown the door. My family wasn't spared. At that realization, I finally remembered—it was my daughter who said talking to me was like talking to a brick wall. I tried to picture her face. I fought back tears. My wife had endured my overbearing ways for years. I thought she'd agreed with me, but she'd only been putting up with me.

My daughter was different. Not just from my wife, but from me as well. Like how Seonsuk grumbled about her son, wondering how someone who came from her could be so different, my daughter and I were polar opposites. From gender to thought processes, interests, and even food tastes, the generational gap was the least of it. She didn't eat meat, showed little interest in studying, and had a gentle disposition, which often left her defenseless against my criticism. When she was younger, she'd at least pretend to listen when she was being scolded, but as a teenager, she began to push back. I couldn't accept that, and my wife became her shield. Back then, I thought my wife's protection was the reason for the communication breakdown between me and my daughter, but now, I see the truth. I was the reason my wife had to become a shield. I was the one who threw away the chance for reconciliation with my daughter that my wife had worked so hard to create. I dismissed my daughter as willful. She treated me as if I were invisible. That was the beginning.

The dissolution of my family, my own downfall, losing my wife and daughter—it was all due to my neglect and arrogance.

Time passed. It was only after I lost my memory to pain, barely managing to open my eyes to the world, that I started to put myself in other people's shoes, to have sympathy, and to connect with others. But by then, there was nobody around me, and it seemed too late to find someone to talk to. Still, I had to keep going. And right now, I needed to help Seonsuk, who was on the verge of falling into the same pit I'd been in. I had to do something, having gone through that agony, having been submerged in that sorrow. That's when Zzamong's words came back to me.

I handed her a triangle gimbap. I suggested she include a letter with the gimbap. And to listen. Just as I'd listened to her, I told her to listen to her son. She nodded, and a wave of embarrassment hit me. Embarrassment and pain because I couldn't write my daughter or listen to her.

After the Lunar New Year, the epidemic that began in China got a lot worse. Infections skyrocketed everywhere, leading to shortages of masks and hand sanitizers. The boss gave me and Seonsuk several masks for our shifts, saying she had stocked up in case the air pollution got bad, since she had a lung condition.

During my night shifts, I didn't mind greeting customers in a mask. After ringing up their purchases, I slathered on hand sanitizer. Even though the situation was new, I found myself adapting easily.

The next day, the boss stressed extra safety and handed out latex gloves. The moment I put them on, it was like lightning flashed through my mind. Remembering the sensation, I squeezed hand sanitizer onto my gloves, rubbed my hands together, then brought them up to my face for a sniff. Even though there were customers around,

I ran from the counter to the mirror wall at the far end of the store. I looked at my reflection. Under my short hair, my V-shaped eyebrows and small eyes seemed to pair perfectly with the mask. Here was a glimpse of my past. The face hidden by the mask, the smell of alcohol from the hand sanitizer, and the familiar feel of the latex gloves were sparking memories of my old life.

I'd been a doctor.

Even now, if I put on a white coat and held a scalpel in my hand, I felt like I could perform any surgery. I could almost smell the disinfectant from the operating room and hear the hum of medical devices surrounding me like background music. I stepped out of the store, like stepping out of an operating room, pulled off my mask, and inhaled the cold air. I had to breathe deeply to keep my memories from shrinking.

Clinging to these memories, I spent days breaking them down and piecing them back together. My brain felt like it was being tickled. The more I uncovered about myself, the more pain, fear, and resistance rose up, but I couldn't stop.

One day, a customer claimed he was the boss's son and tried to walk out without paying for his beer. His eyes and nose, which resembled the boss's, proved he wasn't lying, but I couldn't just let him leave. It was part of my job, and I wanted to show him he wasn't entitled to special treatment here, especially when he never lifted a finger to help. He left in a huff, red in the face, only to come back an hour later. He marched up to me as I was restocking, booze heavy on his breath, and shoved his phone in my face. On the screen was a photo of him grinning with the boss. He asked if that was proof enough, then grilled me about beer sales. I told him the truth. Unhappy with my answer, he grabbed the beer and stalked off. His pathetic behavior reminded me of my brother.

I had an older brother—a real piece of work. We were both smart, but while I used my smarts for academics, he used his for every scam and trick in the book. From early on, he made a living swindling people, and when I got into medical school, he mocked me, asking how much a doctor could even make. He disappeared for a while, only to get in touch years later—probably after spending some time in jail.

The last time I saw him, he showed up at the hospital where I was interning, demanding money and threatening me. I told him that a hospital was filled with scalpels, scissors, poisons—every kind of deadly weapon. Doctors could take lives just as they could save them, and seeing blood was second nature to us. After that, I had no more memories of him.

Yet, as I pieced together my past, the boss's son stirred up memories of my brother. Once his face came to me, so did those of other family members, tangled together like sweet potatoes on a vine. Our mother, from whom we got our brains, left our incompetent father when we were in grade school, placing us in our grandmother's care.

My father worked in construction and was a man of few words. Sometimes he hit us, sometimes he bought us meals, but mostly, he struggled just to take care of himself. Still, seeing that I excelled in my studies, he seemed to hold some hope for me. He sent me to cram schools and gave me an allowance—something he never did for my brother. Like my mother, I moved out as soon as I got into medical school, supporting myself through tutoring. I studied ferociously, trying to erase my father, my brother, and the home we once shared.

I wanted to become a doctor and live in a different world. I dreamed of marrying a woman from a respectable family and starting my own family. And I nearly achieved all of that. But those memories, now surfacing like nightmares, began to haunt me, and I had no way to escape them.

As the mask shortage worsened, people started lining up at pharmacies to buy them. Medical personnel were sent en masse to Daegu, where there had been a massive outbreak. While the world was being turned upside down by COVID-19, I stood masked and lost in thought. Everything was changing—the world and me. The news was filled with heartbreaking stories from Italy, where families couldn't be with their loved ones in their final moments.

In my mind, too, a single thought consumed everything, like the epidemic. Memories, like an infection, told me it was time to return to my real life. It was strange. As death spread, I could see my life more clearly. I had to go find it, even if it meant this would be my final chapter.

I reclaimed my identity and reactivated my dormant social security number, recovering my ID and password, reconnecting to the online world. Had I somehow anticipated this? My cloud storage contained neatly organized records about me—or more accurately, about me and that incident. Grasping the significance of these documents felt as instinctive as if I had been programmed. I did what I had to do.

I sat down with the boss for a talk. She listened as I explained my deeply personal reasons for quitting, and she seemed to understand, at least enough to satisfy her curiosity. She knew all too well that a convenience store was a place where people came and went, where both customers and workers were just passing through to refuel, whether with goods or with money. But at this fueling station, my car had gotten more than just fuel—it had been entirely repaired. And now it was time for me to hit the road again. That's what she seemed to be telling me.

The man tailing me looked to be about sixty. This was my first time being followed, especially in such a clumsy way. As soon as he got on the subway, he sat in the priority seat diagonally across from me, quickly averting his eyes. His profile, surprisingly, reminded me of what I remembered about my father—the large frame, the stubborn expression. Most of all, he seemed to be the age my father was the last time I saw him.

It wasn't until I noticed his resemblance to my father that I naturally figured out who had sent him. Why would someone who acted like my brother bother with something so pointless? Why dig up my past? As annoying as he was, I didn't dislike Kang. Thinking about my father and brother no longer upset me. I glanced at the man tailing me, signaling for him to follow, and got off at Apgujeong Station.

Inside the clinic, I barely recognized any faces. The turnover was high because the director treated the staff like they were disposable medical supplies. Being back here, where I'd once worked, stirred up a flood of memories. I responded curtly to the receptionist who questioned me and headed straight to the director's office.

The director hadn't changed one bit. Even though it had been four years since we last met, he didn't bat an eye and simply asked if I had any thoughts about coming back. When I pointed out the impossibility of working in a clinic that was on the verge of shutting down, he smirked and said I looked like I'd been through some tough times. He added that I might as well go ahead and make another reckless choice if I was set on completely destroying myself.

"You must have been relieved when I vanished . . . but I'm back to expose you . . . and everything that happened here . . . just so we're clear."

"Why? You think blowing the whistle will get you a lighter sentence?"

"You see people as objects . . . useful if they bring in money . . . and trash if they don't."

"That's why I hired you. You had a knack for bringing in money."

"But . . . people aren't like that . . . They're all . . . connected. You can't just separate them whichever way you want . . . and throw them away."

The director sneered and leaned forward.

"So earnest, are we? Fine, my turn to be earnest. After you disappeared, I tried to track you down. I know people who specialize in that sort of thing. But they couldn't find you, so they never got their full fee. But if I tell them you're back and they can get their final payment plus a little extra for their trouble, they'll wrap you up and deliver you right to me. And I'll personally see to your final operation."

I laughed. My cheeks shook as I roared with laughter. The director watched me, unsure if I'd lost it or I was just putting on an act. Watching him squirm only made me laugh harder. Guess villains weren't too fond of happiness. His face twisted in anger.

"You're dead. I'm going to make you pay."

I shrugged. "I've died once already . . . So dying again . . . won't make a difference. I've already reported it . . . These days, shows are always looking for a story like this. So, maybe save that final payment . . . and use it for a lawyer instead."

"You already leaked everything? So you're planning to go down too? Hilarious."

"Like I said . . . I've died . . . once already."

"You're lying. What do you want? A job? You can have your position again. Or is it money?"

"What I want . . . is this."

I showed him my left hand. I'd walked into the clinic wearing latex gloves, and now I spread open my gloved left hand. The director peered at me, trying to figure out what I was getting at. Then I made a fist with my left, grabbed him by the collar with my right, and didn't give him a second to react before hitting him squarely in the face. His head snapped back. I hit him again. When I let go, he collapsed back into his chair, slumped over with his head lolling to the side.

Leaving him writhing in pain, I walked out of the office.

The next morning, just as I was about to leave after my shift, someone called out to me. I turned and saw writer Inkyeong towing her trunk, walking briskly toward the store. She'd been using the apartment across the street as her studio, writing a play. She announced that her first draft was finished, so she was heading back to Daehangno, and gave a big smile. I smiled back. She had been like a counselor to me. Though not an actual psychiatrist, she'd asked probing questions and offered insight. She'd stimulated my brain and played a key role in helping me regain my memories.

"Your play . . . the one you've poured so much into . . . I hope it does well."

"The situation out there is getting worse, so who knows? Just when I finish what might be my life's work, the world goes haywire."

Her eyes sparkled above her mask. Even as she talked about her misfortune, she radiated vitality. Was that the power of someone who lives with dreams? In the early hours at the store, we'd had deep conversations. She'd shared about her own past, helping me dig up mine. I admired her relentless energy for the work she wanted to do. Curious, I'd asked her what drove her. She said life was essentially a series of problems to solve. And since we're solving them anyway, we might as well pick the more interesting ones to tackle.

"Mister, are your memories starting to come back? In my story, the character inspired by you regains his memory."

"Maybe you writing that had something to do with it . . . A lot has come back. Thank you."

She raised her fist—the COVID handshake. I bumped it with mine. I didn't compare the memories she'd written for me with my real ones. We both knew there was no need for that.

Later, the salesman came by a little after ten. He placed a bottle of corn silk tea, somyeon noodles, and some chocolates on the counter. The chocolates were on a buy-one-get-one deal. He grinned at me, and the thought of his twin daughters made me smile. I handed him a note. On it was written the number of Chief Hong from Geukdong Hospital and my real name. He looked puzzled at first, but when I reminded him that he'd mentioned he was in medical equipment sales, adding that dropping my name to Chief Hong might help, he quickly understood. He thanked me over and over, saying he would return the favor if things worked out. I gave him a nod as he left the store.

Earlier that day, I'd reached out to Chief Hong, an old college friend. He was surprised to hear from me, and even more surprised when I referred the salesman. I wasn't sure if he remembered the favor he owed me, or if he still trusted my word, but he promised to give the salesperson a chance. Chief Hong would likely be in for another surprise when he heard about my recent situation from the salesman.

It was the third day of Mr. Kwak's training, and he was fumbling through ringing up a mother and daughter's purchases. Maybe feeling bad for the delay, he called out "Have a nice day!" in a loud voice as they were leaving. The girl, almost out the door, turned, bowed, and replied, "You too." He let out a chuckle, then shot me an embarrassed glance when he noticed me watching.

"I still get mixed up with split transactions. Sorry this old guy's taking so long to catch on."

Why was he sorry? Him taking over the night shift allowed me to quit, and the note he gave me today meant I could finally leave. I pulled up YouTube on the new smartphone I'd gotten that day and found Sihyeon's channel. A new video had been uploaded on ConveniChannel: *Your Convenience Store Guide*. I clicked on "Mastering Split Payments" and handed him the phone. Soon after, he was carefully following Sihyeon's instructions, holding the bar code scanner. It was nice to hear her calm voice again.

"Everyone, this channel may be called ConveniChannel, but let you tell you, working at a convenience store is anything but convenient. It's work, after all. For customers to feel comfortable, we employees have to embrace a bit of discomfort. It took me a whole year to understand this. Even if you're just part time, taking on this discomfort is part of providing great service. And I'll do what I can to make your job a little easier. That wraps up today's ConveniChannel."

I'd intended only to check on how Mr. Kwak restocked the displays, but despite his boasting about working in the Supply Corps during his military days, he made another mistake. I found myself explaining the correct stocking order one more time.

As dawn was breaking, we each had a bowl of instant noodles at the snack bar. Mr. Kwak seemed starved for conversation and rambled on about everything—how decent the boss seemed, how working nights at a convenience store was better than being a security guard. He laughed, asking if I remembered the priceless look on the face of the boss's son the day before. I had to pause and laugh for a while too.

When the boss's son saw Mr. Kwak—the very person he'd hired to drive me out—working at the store, he looked as if he'd seen a ghost. He fired questions at the older man, asking why he was sabo-taging his family's business. Mr. Kwak calmly replied that in South Korea, everyone was free to work where they pleased, and that he had succeeded in driving me away, thus completing his assignment. Livid, the boss's son threw a tantrum, yelling he was going to sell the store, and Mr. Kwak said he'd help the boss keep it open. The situation then escalated, with the owner's son making a scene, and I had to step in. I reminded him that the police station was just five minutes away, and if he wanted to avoid a trip there, he'd better leave. In the end, he stormed out, bitterly complaining that you couldn't trust anyone in this world.

"Now that he's learned a valuable lesson about trust, maybe he'll stop falling for scams," Mr. Kwak mused.

"The day before yesterday the boss was venting to me . . . The brewery her son wanted to take over . . . it turned out to be a scam. He told her they needed to sell the store . . . to finance the business . . . So she looked into it . . . It was a total mess."

"So that's why he lashed out at me," Mr. Kwak said with a chuckle.

"Her son . . . causes her a lot of headaches . . . You've known him for a while . . . Could you keep an eye on him?"

"Sure. In a month or two, he'll probably call me up like nothing happened and say we should grab dinner."

Mr. Kwak gazed out the window as the sun rose, the silhouette of Namsan Tower signaling the start of a new day. He stared at the tower for a while, lost in thought. I finished my noodles and began cleaning up. Suddenly, he turned to me and asked, "Hey, do you have a family?"

He had a lonely look in his eyes. I nodded.

"All my life, I haven't been good to my family. I have so many regrets. Even now, I'm not sure how I should treat them."

I didn't know what to say. His words seemed to be describing me, and I struggled to answer. Seeing my solemn expression, he waved off what he'd just said and turned away with his empty bowl.

"Treat them . . . the way you treat the customers," I finally said.

He looked back in surprise.

"You're kind to customers . . . If you treat your family the same . . . everything will work out."

"Like customers, huh? Maybe I need to learn about hospitality from this place."

Mr. Kwak thanked me and turned around. In the end, weren't family members like customers you meet on life's journey? Treating them with the courtesy we extend to customers, whether they were model ones or pains in the ass, might stop us from hurting each other. I'd just blurted what had come to mind, but I felt relieved my advice seemed to help. But could it apply to me too? Did I even deserve to be a customer?

After overseeing the shift change between Mr. Kwak and Seonsuk, I left the store and headed to Seoul Station. I passed through the station that had once been my home and crossed the plaza to the bus stop. There, a red express bus would take me to my destination. As I waited, I thought about Seonsuk and her son. She had been all smiles today as she told me how they now texted on KakaoTalk. After our conversation that day, she'd written her son a heartfelt letter and given it to him with the triangle gimbap. Soon after, she received a long message from him. He apologized and asked for a little more patience as he figured out what he really wanted to do in life. With that, she was able to restore her faith in him.

She showed me a sticker emoji he'd sent her—a cute little creature sending hearts. I couldn't tell if it was a raccoon or mole, but Seonsuk's happiness was clear.

In the end, life boiled down to relationships, and relationships to communication. Happiness, I realized, wasn't far off. It was in sharing our hearts and minds with those around us. It was something I'd learned over these past months at Always Convenience. No, I'd been learning it slowly over the years at Seoul Station, little by little, as I watched families saying goodbye to their loved ones, lovers reuniting, children accompanying their parents, and friends setting out together . . . I'd watched them, while sitting in my spot on the ground, while talking to myself, while pacing, while wrestling with my thoughts, until finally, I understood.

The express bus traveled for quite some time before entering a small town in southern Gyeonggi-do. Cement mixers and construction trucks barreled down the highway that was still being built, much like the neighborhood it serviced. When the bus dropped me off at one of the stops, it disappeared into the dust, leaving me to walk back to the sign I'd noticed before getting off.

Once I reached the sign, I took a moment to look at it. It said that the Home Memorial Park was five hundred meters away. As I climbed the steep hill, I wondered how to translate the name, which was in English, into Korean. House? Family? Nest? I understood the sentiment behind the name. Home was home. Still, it felt odd that I, a homeless person, was heading to a placed called "home." This was a home where I couldn't belong, in life or in death. But I was here now, and it was time to confront the moment.

I walked past the sculptures at the entrance of the vast park and pulled out the note Mr. Kwak had given me yesterday. After confirming the address, Green A-303, I pulled down my mask and exhaled. Built into a sunny hillside, the memorial park was steep. Alive, I panted, inhaling the crisp air. Maybe because I was at the home of the dead, nobody was around. Since there was no one to give me dirty looks for removing my mask, I stuffed it into my pocket and moved on.

She'd been quite anxious during the consultation. She asked if the surgery would be painful, if there would be any side effects, and whether follow-up procedures would be necessary. I assured her she'd be under general anesthesia, and told her those concerns were more likely to apply to a less reputable hospital on the outskirts of Seoul.

"What you see on the news is on the news for a reason. They're bizarre, rare incidents—that's why they make the news. You've overthinking it. This is Apgujeong. I'm sure you looked us up and saw our reputation, right?"

"You see . . . I've saved up a long time. I can't afford another surgery or follow-up . . . I guess I'm just nervous. It's my first time."

"You came to the right place. This will be your first and last cosmetic surgery, so you don't need to worry. All you need to do is follow the clinic's advice."

"Thanks, I feel a bit better now. Thank you."

A week later, while she was undergoing surgery, I found myself repeating the same words to another patient. Choi, the dentist, was performing the surgery, and I'd observed him for a bit before stepping out for a consultation. The patient, whom I had assured her fears were unfounded, ended up dying while receiving surgery at the hands of a "ghost doctor."

The director acted quickly to handle the incident. Since there was no ghost doctor on record, her death was labeled a medical accident. Her family sued, demanding justice, but when the director leaned on his legal connections, the case didn't even go to prosecution. The matter was closed with a settlement and my resignation. The director told me to take a break until the dust settled, and I had my first real rest in a long time.

Where did it all go wrong?

Was it because I'd allowed a ghost doctor to perform my surgeries? Because I would leave the operating room and let a substitute take over, as if this practice was perfectly acceptable, just so I could see one more client and turn a bigger profit? Because I'd deceived someone who'd looked at me with both worry and hope, trusting me to perform her surgery? Or was it because I worked for a director who only cared about money and routinely ordered ghost surgeries? Was it my shallow ambition, which led me to become a doctor just to climb the social ladder? Or should I blame my early poverty and my incompetent parents, two reasons I vowed to succeed and make a name for myself?

At the time, I couldn't tell. I simply couldn't. Now that I know, I've also realized my actions can't be undone. Standing before Green A-303, before the twenty-two-year-old woman whose life I'd cut short, I used my mask to wipe away tears that wouldn't stop.

I couldn't face this young woman, who'd said she needed to invest in her looks for job interviews, who'd worked part time throughout college to save for cosmetic surgery. She had tried to meet the world's standards to survive, and this effort had sealed her fate. Suddenly, I felt as if the cold blade that had ended her life was still in my hands, and chills ran down my spine.

I fought back tears and reached into my parka. I pulled out not a blade but flowers. They were artificial flowers I had bought yesterday, designed to attach to a surface. I stuck the bright red flowers to her small space. Not knowing what else to do, I stood there. Tears continued to flow.

Hearing footsteps, I covered my mouth with my damp mask and lowered my head. With tears streaming down, I prayed over and over again: I'm sorry . . . I'm truly sorry. Please . . . don't ever forgive me . . . Please . . . rest in peace . . . I truly hope . . . you find peace.

As the express bus entered Seoul, we inevitably hit a traffic jam. I pretended to sleep, my eyes tightly shut, struggling to contain the emotions welling up inside.

My wife didn't buy my vague claim of being on paid leave. She kept pressing for details, wanting to know the full story. I'd learned to be brazen and unapologetic in these situations, so I brushed her off, saying I was having a conflict with the director and needed some time off. But this pretense didn't last long. The volunteer group the deceased had been part of showed up at the clinic, staging a protest. The incident quickly caught media attention and spread online.

My wife demanded the truth. I dodged her questions. Did the truth matter that much? To protect my family and myself, keeping quiet was the only option. But my wife kept pushing, saying that even our daughter was curious about the incident. Wasn't that more reason to keep quiet and deny everything? Frustrated, I told her I hadn't caused the medical accident. It had happened under Dr. Seo's watch, plus these things happened in our line of work. The director was skilled at handling such crises, I assured her, and I would return to work soon. I was simply taking a break from the chaos at the clinic.

My wife remained unconvinced but stopped with the questions. She started coming home late, visiting temples to pray or wandering aimlessly. The strained atmosphere at home drove my daughter to keep her distance as well. So, on a Sunday night, as I lay alone at home, waiting for a food delivery, I snapped. I called my wife and ranted the moment she picked up. Did she think I was enjoying this? That working at that clinic wasn't eating me up inside? I was putting up with it for their sake, to give them a good life. How else were we supposed to live? Life wasn't easy. There were always losers and victims, and I was breaking my back for this family. And now she couldn't be supportive when I needed a break? Where the hell was she anyway? She needed to come home this minute!

Late that night, my wife and daughter returned, looking defeated. My wife suggested we take some time, promising not to bring up the hospital incident until it was resolved. I agreed and looked at my daughter, expecting her to understand. But she, who was unlike me in every way, stared back at me with her small eyes—the only feature she had inherited from me, and the one I despised most in myself. *If only she had inherited her mother's eyes instead.* Before I knew it, the words slipped out of my mouth: "Listen, when you get into college, I'll pay for your double eyelid surgery."

"Why? You want to kill me too?"

Her response stunned both me and my wife. My whole body started to tremble, but my daughter glared at me, refusing to look away. Without thinking, I raised my hand. At that moment, my wife stepped between us. She shouted at me, blocking me with her body, but nothing she said registered. Shaking with rage, I tried to lunge at my daughter, but my wife pushed me back. I shoved her aside. She crashed into the cabinet with a sharp cry and fell to the floor.

When I came to my senses, my daughter was sitting next to my fallen wife, frantically dialing for help. All I could do was sit there, dumbfounded by the scene before me.

The doctor treated her injuries and said she needed a few days of rest, recommending she be admitted to the hospital. My wife, lying in a private room, stared blankly at the ceiling, avoiding my gaze. No matter how much I apologized and promised that nothing like this would happen again, she remained silent. She turned her back to me and looked out the window. Sitting by her bedside, I scrubbed my face, fought back tears, and lowered my head.

How much time passed before I heard her voice?

"Did you actually think you were taking care of us?"

I looked up at her haggard face against the hospital pillow.

"Taking care of us . . . you don't need to do that anymore."

"What do you mean?"

She closed her eyes. I sat there, breathing heavily, saying nothing.

"If you truly cared, you would have been honest."

She was asking for the truth. But I couldn't respond. I couldn't bring myself to confess, fearing her judgment. So I stayed quiet.

Days later, my wife seemed to return to normal. She was more reserved, but I believed things would get better in time. Just then, I received a call from the clinic to return to work, and I went back, as if nothing had happened.

When I got home, my wife and daughter were gone.

That was the end.

It was the end for me too. They had vanished without a trace, and they didn't answer my calls. I had tried to build a family of my own, different from the miserable home of my youth, but now everything was in ruins. I couldn't sleep without drinking myself into oblivion.

When I failed to show up at work for a few days, the director called. I ranted into the phone about how my family had fallen apart and how I was teetering on the brink of madness. The director scoffed and told me to take a permanent break. He must have thought I'd finally lost it. But I was determined to make him pay, this director who had treated me like a fool, to drag him down to hell with me if necessary, to somehow compensate for my shattered life.

I collected all the documents on the clinic's corruption and uploaded them to a cloud account. At the same time, I continued to search for my wife and daughter. But I was slowly coming undone. As I dug deeper into the corruption, I had to confront my own shame, and the guilt I felt toward my family intertwined with the guilt over the patient I had killed. It suffocated me. The agony became unbearable, and I was disgusted with myself. Alcohol became my only refuge. I had to stay drunk constantly, eventually becoming incapable of functioning in daily life. I reached a point where I needed to find myself before finding my wife and daughter again.

When I finally learned they were in Daegu, I was dying in a house plastered with foreclosure signs. Gathering the last of my strength, I packed my bags and headed to Seoul Station. As I held a KTX ticket to Daegu, the mere thought of facing my wife and daughter sent me into a panic. I broke out in a cold sweat. I tore up the ticket and backed away. I ran to the bathroom, vomited, and then collapsed.

When I woke up, everything was gone except for the pants and T-shirt I had on. My expensive jacket, bespoke shoes, wallet, and bag had long been stolen. Standing barefoot, I stared into the bathroom mirror. I saw my wife and daughter in the reflection, but as soon as their faces morphed into mine, I smashed my head into the glass.

After that, I couldn't leave Seoul Station. People called me homeless, and fellow homeless people knew me as Dokgo. It was the name of a dead old man.

When I arrived at Seoul Station, I made my way to Hoehyeon-dong and checked into a motel with a bathtub. I filled the tub with hot water and soaked my body. As sweat started to bead on my forehead, I sipped corn silk tea. After finishing all four bottles I'd brought, I gave myself a thorough scrub. Then, I took another shower, brushed my teeth, and lay down on the bed to sleep.

The next morning, I woke up, got dressed, and went out. I was hungry, but an empty stomach didn't feel too bad. Once I started emptying myself, I felt I could go days without eating, and I believed it would help clear my mind.

As I approached Seoul Station, my heart began to race. After crossing several traffic lights, I reached the station plaza, where an organization was distributing masks to the homeless. Seeing the homeless in masks was an odd sight. Were the masks for their protection, or to prevent them from spreading disease? Probably both. With masks on, we all looked the same—potential carriers and sources of infection. We were a virus called humans, the same virus that has plagued the Earth for tens of thousands of years.

Buying a ticket to Daegu brought back memories of my breakdown here four years ago. This time, though, I wasn't alone. I saw the boss, holding a convenience store plastic bag, walking toward me. She'd insisted on seeing me off, saying that since we met at Seoul Station, it was only fitting to say goodbye here. To be honest, I desperately needed her help. A part of me hoped she would stop me if I tore up my ticket again and ran to the bathroom to smash my head into the mirror.

"I brought your favorites," she said.

She handed me the plastic bag with an Ultimate Feast Lunch Box and a bottle of corn silk tea. For a moment, I was speechless, and could only stare at the bag.

"Once you're in Daegu, you'll be able to prove you're a doctor, right?"

"I've already confirmed it over the phone . . ."

In this country, killing someone or committing a sexual crime didn't cost you your medical license. That's why it was dubbed a "Phoenix license." Why? Because doctors were usually buddies with lawmakers. Maybe this terrible privilege of saving or ending lives deluded us into seeing ourselves as gods. After one of my patients made it big as a celebrity, people said she'd been touched by a "medical god." But I was just a person. An arrogant, no-good, selfish one at that.

"I didn't want to let you go, but how could I stop you? Especially now when they need your help. Having watched you all this time, I know you'll do well over there. Take care, okay?"

"It's all . . . because of you. If I hadn't met you . . . I'd still be lying here . . . instead of going to Daegu."

"So, I guess I'm joining the fight against COVID too?"

"Definitely."

I'd never volunteered for anything as a doctor, but here I was, off to Daegu to provide medical support. I thought again of my patient in the columbarium I had visited yesterday. No, going to Daegu wouldn't make up for what I'd done, but it was a step toward living with my guilt. And I had to keep taking those steps.

"With everyone in masks, the world has gotten pretty quiet, don't you think?" the boss said.

"Sure has."

"People like to blab. The world isn't a high school classroom, but they talk loudly, acting like they have it all figured out. Maybe the Earth spread this plague to shut humans up."

"But some won't wear masks . . . and they don't stop yapping," I said.

"Exactly. Those ones need a beating, if you ask me."

"Yes . . . Ha ha." I couldn't help chuckling.

"Complaining about masks, about COVID, about how everything's a hassle," she said. "They say they have the right to do whatever they want, but hey, that's not how life works. Life's not meant to be comfortable and convenient all the time."

"Looks that way."

"Hey, did you know? People used to call our store the 'Inconvenience Store.'"

"You knew?"

"Yup. We had less variety and fewer sales than other stores. And we weren't a neighborhood corner store where you could bargain, so I guess that made us 'inconvenient.'"

"The Inconvenience Store . . ."

"Then when you showed up, things got a bit easier for everyone. But looks like we're going back to being the Inconvenience Store."

"Why's that?"

"Because you're leaving. When you finish your business in Daegu, make sure you come back."

I offered an awkward smile. The boss hit me playfully on the back.

"Never mind. What did I say earlier? People need to experience a little discomfort. So maybe it's good for our store to become inconvenient again. Don't you dare come back."

"All right."

"And don't just focus on volunteer work. Make sure you see your family too."

Did I ever tell her my family was in Daegu? Or was my memory slipping again?

It seemed the boss resembled the god she worshipped. How else could she understand and look after me like this? In this world, those we called "medical gods" weren't the ones who were divine. It had to be people like her, full of compassion and empathy.

It was almost time to leave, but I couldn't move. I was rooted to the spot, as if an invisible magnet was pulling me back. I stood there, anxious, feeling as though the boss were my lifeline.

"Go on now. I can't keep standing here forever."

I turned to face her. Was she the mother who'd left? Or the caring grandmother who'd looked after me until she passed away? Who was she?

"I should have died, but you saved me," I mumbled, hugging her. "I'm ashamed, but . . . I'll try to carry on."

She didn't say anything. She just patted my back with her small hand.

As soon as I passed the ticket gate, I hurried to the platform without looking back. After boarding the train and settling into my seat, tears began to flow. I hoped the train would start moving. I hoped it would go so fast that my tears would be swept away, whisking me to Daegu in no time. As if it knew my wish, the train began to move. As we left Seoul Station, I could almost see the path to the convenience store outside the window. It seemed I could even see the green hills of Cheongpa-dong and the store that was anything but convenient.

The train began to cross the Hangang Bridge. The water sparkled and danced in the morning sunlight.

Though I said I hadn't left Seoul Station since becoming homeless, I'd actually gone to the Han River once. I'd climbed onto the bridge, intending to throw myself off, but I hadn't been able to follow through. In fact, after this winter, I had planned to jump from the Mapo Bridge or Wonhyo Bridge. But now, I understood.

The river was for crossing, not for plunging into.

A bridge was for getting to the other side, not for leaping off.

My tears wouldn't stop. I was ashamed, but I resolved to live. I decided to bear my guilt. I would offer help when necessary, share what I could, and not live solely for myself. I would use my skills, once meant only for my survival, for the benefit of others. I would seek out my family and apologize. If they refused to see me, I would respect their decision and live with the consequences. Holding on to the belief that life had meaning and must go on, I, too, would carry on.

The train crossed the river, and with that, my tears stopped.

About the Author

Kim Ho-Yeon has worked as a novelist, screenwriter, and comic book author. Considered a complete storyteller, he won the 9th Segye Literary Prize (offered by the *Segye Times* newspaper) in 2013, and in 2021, was awarded Yes24 Book of the Year and Millie Audiobook of the Year. His work stands out for the humanity conveyed by his characters, always inspiring, and for stories that remind us of our own lives. He lives in Seoul.

About the Translator

Janet Hong is a writer and translator based in Vancouver, Canada. She received the TA First Translation Prize and the LTI Korea Translation Award for her translation of Han Yujoo's *The Impossible Fairy Tale*. She is also a two-time winner of the Harvey Award for Best International Book for her translations of Keum Suk Gendry-Kim's *Grass* and Yeong-shin Ma's *Moms*. Recent translations include Hwang Jungeun's *Years and Years* and Kwon Yeo-sun's *Lemon*.